# Odin's Story: Book of Urd

Book 1 of Odin's Sacred Runes

Nathan Anderson

Edited by Nicole Jakub, J.T. Zaglas, F. Nordhagen &

Z. Markel

Book cover artwork: DC Wince

Copyright © 2022 Nathan Anderson

All rights reserved.

ISBN:9798410532617

# CONTENTS

| C | Title | P | C | Title | P | C | Title | P |
|---|---|---|---|---|---|---|---|---|
| 1 | Introduction | 8 | 14 | A Son's Rise | 54 | 27 | Love and Hate | 100 |
| 2 | A Weary Wanderer | 10 | 15 | The Bear and the Raven | 57 | 28 | In the Shadows | 103 |
| 3 | In the Beginning | 12 | 16 | Family Reunion | 60 | 29 | Quenching a Thirst | 106 |
| 4 | Vixen | 16 | 17 | Three Bother's Return Home | 64 | 30 | Blood is Thicker than Water | 110 |
| 5 | Gift of Wisdom | 19 | 18 | Gift for a Gift | 67 | 31 | Mysterious Stranger | 114 |
| 6 | Building the Village | 24 | 19 | Return of the Yulefather | 70 | 32 | Heavy is the Head | 118 |
| 7 | A Father's Tears | 30 | 20 | Need is Better than Desire | 75 | 33 | Best Laid Plans | 122 |
| 8 | Burning of Gulveig | 33 | 21 | Travelling Far and Wide | 78 | 34 | Deceiving Gunlodd | 127 |
| 9 | No Peace Without War | 36 | 22 | A Gift to Make Amends | 82 | 35 | The Star on the Tree | 131 |
| 10 | The Wandering Dead | 40 | 23 | Cost of the Silk Ribbon | 84 | 36 | The Riddle Weaver | 135 |
| 11 | Show of Strength | 43 | 24 | Gathering of Friends and Family | 89 | | | |
| 12 | Rise of Donar | 47 | 25 | Sigurd's Destiny | 93 | | | |
| 13 | Angerboda's Brood | 51 | 26 | Dragon Slayer | 96 | | | |

# Dedicated to

This book is dedicated to Kelly Nicholson. You have shown me the true meaning of strength. It is not how much weight you can lift, or how many burdens you can carry. True strength is how you carry yourself while being presented with a multitude of things that would break most people down. You continue to inspire me in this little journey called life.

# ACKNOWLEDGMENTS

Padraic Colum and PogányW. (2019). *The children of Odin: the book of northern myths*. New York, N.Y.: Aladdin

Snorri Sturluson and Arthur Gilchrist Brodeur (2010). *The prose edda: tales from Norse mythology*.

Larrington, C. (2019). *Poetic Edda.* Oxford University Press.

Saxo, G. and Hansen, W.F. (1983). *Saxo Grammaticus & the life of Hamlet: a translation, history, and commentary*. Lincoln: University Of Nebraska Press.

Reaves, W.P. (2018). *Odin's Wife*. Amazon: KDP self-publishing, p.363

# Introduction

Mythology is an exciting spin to transform a simple story into something epic. Since I was a child, mythology has been of interest to me. Ancient tales of gods and demigods challenging giant monsters make everyday life seem dull and mundane in comparison. It wasn't until my 30's that I decided to wonder, in-depth, about the spiritual meaning behind myths. Whether it be a story of a god or a heroic human with god heritage, what could the life application be? Beyond entertainment, religion is a tool used to guide those on living.

The characters in a game ignited my curiosity about Norse Mythology. Magni and Modi, the sons of Thor, took me into a deep dive into Norse myths. An actual YouTube wormhole with multiple different telling's of similar tales, with the death of Ymir to the inevitable Ragnarök and beyond. Myths and folklore that spread all across the world, with every variant of similar stories that painted a vivid picture that got me asking, why? what purpose could grown people have to believe in such stories? Was it for explaining weather, or was it explaining internal human natures by relating them to the outside world?

After about two years of deciphering the fragmented pieces of the Poetic and Prose Edda, I started to look into other sources. Children of Odin, Neil Gaimon, Jackson Crawford, with his linguistic translations, all appeared to hint at a much larger plotline. Discussions with reconstructionists and spiritualists from all different backgrounds led to my theories of plotlines. It all became clear with stories containing number patterns, character links through religious practices and descriptions. We have a lot of information but no real clue.

Snorri's structuring of his Edda has a beginning, end and then everything in between. This method was to depict the storyline as cyclical. He was relating the battle of Ymir to something similar to Ragnarök. The Saxo Grammaticus depicts Odin as Loki from an outward perspective. This was easy to do, as they both share shapeshifting abilities and deceive others. However, painting a leader of a religious pantheon a villain didn't sit right with me. The more I had dived into the lore, the more questions I had.

Taking a break from the Norse myth, I began to look into other regional tales. Whether it was Slavic creatures, Celtic fae, Greek heroes and even the similarities in Egyptian gods and goddesses, it all started to point to one truth. These probably, at one point, were the same. Tales change, names change and even religion changes. But every variant from Aboriginal to Chinese myths share similarities. I decided to stick to the Norse storyline. I have put together a potential tale but found a way to incorporate other myths and folklores within the story and plotlines.

In no way am I saying my book references the source information. It is simply an entertaining way to present an abundance of information through the eye of a leader of gods, a father of many and a husband with faults. I'm not perfect, but neither is Odin, and that is the truth of it all. Take in everything, cut out the noise and walk your path. Do not make assumptions based on small facts but realise the truth. The world is perceptual, and we understand things in our own way.

# A Weary Wanderer

To whomsoever reads this, wherever you may be, greetings to you, I have arrived. Where shall I sit? Only a fool would rely on luck when being hosted by a stranger. Warmth and comfort are needed for legs that are numb. Food and clean clothes are necessary for those that have wandered far in mind and on land. Gracious host, allow me to make myself presentable. May we share courteous words and silence so I may tell my tale?

I know a lot, including you. But knowledge does not determine the value of a person. Instead, I share only what is needed. That is the reason I will rarely make mistakes. Know that I do not talk much, but when I do, you had better listen. My name is unimportant; my role is not your concern. I am simply a weary old man that requires some hospitality in exchange for a grand tale to tell. Would you be so kind as to share your time with a tired old man?

Over the millennia that humans have been on the planet, they have become more segregated by culture and diversity rather than unity; by mythologies and folklore of people spanning from Egypt to Scandinavia and none have paid attention. When three, I and my two brothers, defeated a titan to claim control of the world and I conquered Ymir to make the world. Horus was the Egyptian name I used when I lost my eye to my uncle. However, in Scandinavia I sacrificed mine to my uncle for wisdom.

From Anubis to Cerberus, each culture linked dogs to death. It is only fitting that I meet my end from a giant monstrous wolf.

From the lochs of Scotland to the landscape of Australia and everywhere in between, all over the world shares a connection through the gods and representation of beings far superior to themselves. The truth is, I have gone by many names, but so have many other characters from the origin of Paganism. Languages evolve, tongues change from region to region.

I was the falcon-headed hero of Egypt. In Greece, I was the promiscuous eagle that had many mortal children, and in Norway, I was the flock of ravens that feasted on the dead. In each country, birds have always been my favourite form, as there is freedom in the skies above, flying over obstacles and gaining a better perspective on what appears below. My power of transformation into birds links me to the ruling of the skies.

Make yourself comfortable and grab yourself a drink. I am about to explain everything.

# In The Beginning

Now to tell this extraordinary tale of mine. I will take you back to before I came into this life I have now. Years ago, is an understatement, but those that seek to change, should wander. Those ignorant to possibility should remain in their comfort. Foolish, ignorant people appear when sitting with wiser folk.

Long ago, when time and life was nothing, two elemental forces existed: one of smouldering and skin-blistering heat and the other was cold, with icy winds and blizzard-like mists making it impossible to see anything ahead. And then, there was Ginnungagap: a vast emptiness where nothing existed between the two elements.

As the cold mists from Niflheim crept slowly to the centre of the void, a large ice block emerged. As Niflheim expanded into the empty nothingness around the block, all seemed lost. Before long, there was ice and snow as far as the eyes could see.

Meanwhile, in a mountain of lava far away in the heart of Muspelheim, deep beneath the immense heat and scorching sands, an egg began to hatch. An egg so small, but sometimes, even the small have enough power to ignite the passion of self-discovery. A tiny dragon emerged amongst the flame and ash; a celebration of the first life to come into existence.

Blazing fires and sparks danced in the place where the rivers flowed with smouldering magma. A celebration of the first life to come into existence. The young dragon, Nidhoggr, harmless at first, would be the beginning of everything. Spitting embers and flames in its youth, he would cause of the unveiling of the primordial entities in the space between the two realms. His breath would fight the ice advancing from Niflheim.

The enormous block of ice from Niflheim began to melt, unveiling something colossal. Ymir was the first to emerge. A Giant of Giants, this titan would lay amongst the snow receiving the heat from the far-off land of Muspelheim to keep him warm. If I was to relate this place to something similar to today's world it would have to be the Sahara Desert.

The second creature to appear would be the great cow Audumla. From her four tits, the milk would provide Ymir's nourishment for sustenance. She was enormous, and it was her that unveiled the third.

Buri was the progenitor of the Aesir. Buri was my grandfather, and he was a quiet, cold and controlling man. He planned and structured things to play out as he decided with little influence to sway the outcomes. In the end, I would share the most likeness to him.

Buri gave birth to Bor, my father. He was the warrior. As strong as my son Thor, he wielded an axe like no other. As the flames from Muspelheim continued to drift across the land once known as Ginnungagap, the icy landscape began to warm further. The dragon's breath caused Ymir to sweat. His perspiration gave birth to the first of the Jotuns. Initially, this gave birth to few. Bolthorn came as the first generation of monsters from Ymir's armpits, making Ymir our mother's grandfather. Our uncle Mimir and mother Bestla would have been the first to be birthed becoming the second generation of Jotun.

My mother, Bestla, was harsh but loving. She raised three boys: Vili, Ve and I. Everything she had done has a lesson and a reason behind her actions.

Mimir, our uncle, was wise. It was as if he had already experienced everything, we wished to experience ourselves. As with every action, every mistake my brothers and I made, he would be three steps ahead of every plan we seized. We were young, but with our uncle as a teacher, we would always strive for more.

Before our family would begin to rise to power, the world had yet to finish evolving. As the flames from Nidhoggr drifted in all directions, some floated up to create the stars, and with a large clearing of his throat, the sun was created. With heat emitting from above and below, the warming of Ginnungagap became alarming. Ymir began to sweat more, but this was no normal perspiration. This sweat would give birth to a significant number of creatures: giants, trolls, ogres, six-headed monsters who would destroy one another.

Chaos ensued, establishing a considerable uncertainty of what was to be. The only control over their numbers would be Ymir's footsteps. He would trample all without care or notice of any forms of life. He was chaos personified and every moment was a matter of survival.

Overtime, I, along with my brothers, decided enough was enough. This began an epic battle between the forces of chaos and our attempts to grasp control and order. Buri fell first, charging in to protect us, but sadly was consumed by the masses of Jotun forces. Mimir was quick to rise and slay all that consumed our grandfather. He was such an epic slayer and a great warrior. His trusty footwear shielded him somewhat from stepping over the sharpened weapons of the Jotuns.

My father, Bor, dropped trolls and ogres by the hundreds, giving us time to act. As Jotun armies fell, so did my father from wounds he received in his mighty battle. He walked nine steps, never to rise again.

Vili, Ve and I approached the great Ymir nervously. The smallest of his toes were the size of a large hill. We had to proceed; it was our only chance. Scaling up his large body provided even more danger. The air was thin, his body hair stood as tall as the pine trees and his perspiration gave us an avalanche of monsters to fight. When we reached the head, the frost and ice surrounding his horn made it difficult to steady ourselves. However, with sword, spear and axe, we fought bravely. We were hacking away while the screams echoed throughout the darkness. Our arms were heavy after our many attacks that caused the titan's bitter blood to burst from the open wounds. The salty ocean of blood consumed everything on the battlefield, which marked the end of the time of Ymir.

The great cow disappeared beneath the waves leaving nothing but sand and heat of Muspelheim and the icy landscape of Niflheim once more. This time was different because it wasn't nothingness between the two terrains. Upon observing the new landscape, my brothers and I were knee-deep in Jotun blood and watched as the seas began to rise. We knew then that if we were to pursue a journey, it would be an incredible seaworthy voyage.

Mimir agreed as he pulled us onto one of Audumla's horns she had shed. We then proceeded to float aimlessly over troubled waters. This great battle that changed things exhausted my brothers and me. We welcomed the seemingly endless drifting at sea momentarily to recover.

The flood of Ymir's blood did not claim all Jotun life, though few creatures survived the massacre, including four Jotuns (my mother and uncle in that count), amongst the bloodshed. Our mother remained in Niflheim, and our uncle Mimir would dedicate his remaining time to continue teaching wisdom to my brothers and me, meaning he would join us on this journey. The other two Jotuns drifted across the vast oceans, though our paths would later cross once more.

Ymir's rotten flesh attracted some maggots that my brothers and I would later create the elves with. This species would exist mainly in animal form to the human eye and would be the progenitors of dwarves, goblins, fairies, nymphs and noble elven warriors. For a time, there would be quiet and rest, but there was still so much to accomplish.

"I am the eldest, so the title of ruler and king of gods should be mine, and mine alone," Vili claimed.

"I will take second in line!" Shouted Ve eagerly.

Silence fell across my face, for already they wished kingship, even though all that existed was a land covered in blood and death. Mimir watched our actions and listened to our words. He seen the reflection of a similar dispute in times past. "Perhaps we should work on what you wish to rule," Mimir interrupted the two fools.

"We need to decide on what it is that each of us truly wants and what we are willing to sacrifice to obtain it," I suggested profoundly.

We began to sail across the ocean of blood in hopes of finding more but went decades without finding anything. Then in the distance, when we stared into the crisp ocean spray, a hand barely breached the surface. It was so far on the horizon that only Ve and I could see with our enhanced vision. The hand was dainty and delicate as a beautiful rose, but each rose has its thorns. Vili steered the ship towards the delicate flower.

"The prize is mine!" he claimed as the eldest. He leant over the boat's bow and reached to grab it. He heaved and he pulled, but the maiden's hand was stuck as if her freedom was being hindered by something or someone. My brother and I aided Vili with all our might and after we struggled, there she was, accompanied by something we hadn't seen before: the most beautiful of maidens, with her flowing red hair draping down her back like autumn leaves falling in the wind. Her eyes were as green as the grassy meadows in the spring. She was a beauty like no other, only surpassed by the feeling of her hidden power.

As she emerged from the water, with her came a land that elevated my brothers and me above the blood of Ymir, creating sure footing after drifting lost among the vast seas. With our feet planted firmly on the ground, so began the courting of a princess of Vanaheim.

# Vixen

My brothers were taken by the lady's beauty first. The bumbling fools claimed greatness but acted childishly. They were fascinated with her by her appearance, and I couldn't blame them. Her beauty was enough to snare the loosest tongue. It was years of exploration on the great ocean without bearing any fruitful plunder, therefore coming upon her was a sight that was more than welcome.

Think before you pursue desires, host. Judgement belongs to you alone. It will only bring sadness to want something you cannot have; to love one not faithful to you is like balancing on ice. They will leave you in troubled waters trying to grasp your inner strength with a crippled hand. Bravely, those shall speak to win a heart. Gift your time often, compliment their beauty. Those with experience in this will win the hand of another.

Once we stepped onto land after snatching her from the cold and bitter grasp of the ocean, we became bewitched by her beauty. "My name is Jord," the words trickled from her mouth and took hold of our hearts. "I have only three nights of freedom before my Jotun sisters would take me home once more."

The first night Vili and Ve tripped over themselves. They both ravaged her beyond the trees as I regretfully stepped away from my elder brothers. She seemed like she was in control of the situation, though. The sound of her whispers delicately trickled to my ears as they floated on the air from beyond the trees. I could not make out the enchantment, but it did intrigue me enough to drive me to try to learn such a spell.

The second day, I began to enquire more. I asked where she came from and about her home. She began to inform me first of her mother and father, Aegir and Ran. They were the Jotuns born of Ymir's blood. Greedy and torturous rulers of the deep, they gave the magical creation of fish, whales and all kinds of marine life. Jord had many sisters: nine wave maidens, Sif, Idunn, Gulveig and almost every female warrior of Vanaheim.
Suddenly, I was curious about this magic I had overheard her chanting and asked her more. I wanted to know everything about her land, the beings and her life. "You are not like your brothers," she said, taken by my eagerness to learn more about her.

Next, she told me of her sisters, the wave maidens. Each of these beautiful maidens escaped temporarily, from time to time, making it to shore, only to be dragged back by their mother. It was apparent that in all these years of exploring the vastness of the ocean, there was more than what appeared on the surface. We had never come across such enchanting and intriguing people that lived in this place called Vanaheim.

She continued to talk through the day, I found it curious that there were only two males that existed in Vanaheim. King Aegir, her father, was a cruel tyrant of the sea, but her brother to be a more substantial ruler. He seemed to be calmer of spirit and more peaceful in nature. He was a young prince but with a bit of guidance from the right person, he could become a great ally.

"How do I get there?" I asked eagerly.

"You can't. Vanaheim comes to those who are ready for it." This lack of control had me curious and eager to prove her wrong. I was rash in my younger days. We spent all day talking and I fell hard. Love has a way of bringing a warrior to their knees but also gives them a reason to fight in the first place.

"You must wait, Odin. Wait for dark. If you want me, come secretly. If your brothers knew of our union, it would be unlucky for you." A passion burned inside of me. I left her thinking I had won her hand and heart that night, but I was wrong.

As I later waited in the reeds, hoping to lay with her, the secrecy made me desire the lady's touch more. I attempted to return to Jord's side later that night in the stealthiest manner while the fire my brothers had conjured was dancing in the darkness and while the air was filled with echoes of laughter and boasts. I couldn't continue to Jord's encampment and remain undiscovered. I retreated to the reeds once more.

As the sun rose when all slept, I managed to slip past my brothers, but I found another tied to her bed. Had I not spent all day yesterday getting to know her? I felt I knew her, but not as much as I believed. "What is this?" I asked, puzzled.

"I enjoyed our chat today, however, my legs remain closed to you, for now, Odin." I stayed quiet while the shock of it all ran across my face.

"Who is this tied to your bed?" I asked.

She replied, "Your prize, my love. Her name is Sif. She is a sister of mine and will teach you much."

I was hesitant to perform on a tied-up maiden, even one as beautiful as Sif, as I only desired to be with Jord. I enacted the magic of Seidr as instructed by her. Learning fertility through the actions of making love in another's embrace made me love Jord more still. That maiden taught me a lesson. Her craftiness covered me in shame, but it wasn't all I got from the lady. I learned the magic behind fertility.

During my instructed performance, Jord spoke the magical incantations involved in Seidr. Her words were fair, although her echoes of chants in the wind repeated like the night before when my brothers had their way. Foolishly and unlike me, they did not learn much.

This magic was specific to female Jotun witches, known as Volvas and was the magic of creation. Jord used it to conceive two creatures: one of Vili's seed and the other of Ve's. Unknown to them, it was the duplicity of the two that would make the world a fascinating place to be.

Inside Sif's belly, there was a child of mine. I explored her body to learn the magic of Seidr. I took in everything; the chant, the actions performed, and the most subtle details to perform the spell.

On the third day, Jord and Sif returned with three children: two wolf pups and a bear cub. Vili had a wolf son called Geri and Ve had a wolf daughter called Freki. They were skinny runts of beasts, but my nephew and niece had my love and respect Immediately.

I called my bear cub son, Ullr. He stomped toward me with power and might. He was strong and well-tempered compared to his wolf cousins.

The sisters then left, stepping into the water and disappearing in an instant. Just like that, Jord was gone. Nowhere in sight, but just before she departed, she whispered in my ear, "You must free us from my mother and father." The Vanir wave maidens dragged her back into the cold depths of the ocean once more.

# Gift of Wisdom

We met Mimir and sailed our ship towards Niflheim. However, we came across an unusual land. There was rocky terrain and barren mountains that felt hostile. Like most youths, my brothers and I began to explore this realm that had trees so tall, they would scrape the clouds like fingers dragging through the winter snow. They were dark, malevolent and sinister that had no leaves. There were no signs of green grass, just tall, gloomy forests blocking the light from the sun forged from Muspelheim.

We journeyed through the mysterious lands; and we climbed the highest mountains to observe the grounds. To the west were the trolls, to the east, there were ogres. In the north, there were giants and to the south were a variety of Jotuns. Similar to the time of Ymir. These creatures varied in size and shape. "This is Jotunheim," I declared.

"We need to destroy them, brothers!" the foolish Vili exclaimed.

"Why would we?" Ve asked curiously.

"We do not quarrel with these beings. Ymir is gone. Life can now flourish. There is more than enough room for these beings. They have not wronged us and they, too, deserve a chance to live in peace," I announced.

"I am king, and I am not taking instruction from another who couldn't woo Jord, oh wise one. A fool avoids a battle in hopes he'll live forever. Old age will show you no kindness if you avoid the fight, brother." Vili angrily told me. Unknown to us, someone approached from behind while they argued. With a quick slap on the back of his head, Vili was silenced.

"It isn't wise to mock another while they suffer. Love makes fools of the wise and if you think all Jotuns should die, what of me, Boy! Think before you speak, foolish Vili. What you want and what you get is dependent on the words you speak about the destruction of Jotun blood." Instructed Mimir to his young nephews. A dumb silence fell on Vili's face. "A person is known by their speech to another, Vili. The foolish should remain quiet. What and how did these lands come to be?" Mimir asked. We informed him of everything that happened with Jord. "Hmmm, interesting, and what did we learn of such things?" Mimir quizzed my brothers and me.

"Sex is great!" Vili proclaimed ignorantly.

"The ignorant think all who laugh with him are a friend. Unaware when they sit with the wise how they speak of them," Mimir replied.

"Sex is fun!" Ve said with the goofiest smile across his face.

"The fool thinks they know all. But when tested by the wise, it is proven how foolish they are. And what did you learn?" Mimir turned to me, expecting another dumb answer.

"Seidr magic, the ability to create new things to manipulate fate in the slightest. Is that correct, uncle?" I replied hesitantly.

"To ask and answer honestly identifies the wise. The telling of all, so nothing remains hidden. Well done, boy. Perhaps there is hope for the realms yet," Mimir cracked the smallest of grins. If it weren't for my all-seeing eyes, I would have missed the subtle expression. "We can't simply destroy an entire race because they are different. I am a Jotan, and these lands are populated by the descendants of Bergelmir and his wife. My nieces and nephews, the grandchildren of the high and mighty Ymir himself. The mountains you climbed in this land are Ymir's bones. These beings might hold ill will toward you for the death of the great titan. No one trusts another who has harmed someone they have loved before. A broken home does not provide shelter and a horse with a lame leg is not to be trusted. Let me take you to the king and queen of this great land. Vili, you should remain silent. All will know of your stupidity the more you talk," Mimir said, clear and proud of his heritage. "Ve, even the greatest of chiefs are willing to give something important to keep the peace in what kingdom they have created."

As we approached the Jotun encampment hesitantly, we were snarled, grunted and roared at by each type of Jotun. My hand firmly gripped my spear, but I did not act rashly. The wise guest remains unmoved when being taunted by a host. Their actions speak much of their dishonourable character. My brothers lifted axe and sword in defence of such intimidation. "Lower your weapons, boys," Mimir instructed as we all entered the throne of the king and queen of Jotunheim.

"Ah, uncle Mimir, nice to see you after such a long time," Bergelmir welcomed us all into his hall. The Jotun prepared a feast, and much discussion happened between them all. I remained silent and respectful, but my brothers ignorantly boasted of Ymir's defeat and made jokes about his features as he died.

"Ah yes, those with a gluttonous ego consume too much self-praise, only to be mocked for a swollen head and a bloated belly," Mimir calmed the tension between the host and silenced my brothers.

"You do not say much, Odin. Is your tongue filled with poisonous words like your brothers?" Asked the king.

"I do not wish to be disrespectful in someone's house when I am the guest. I would enjoy your tale of how you discovered these lands, only if you would be so kind as to share it, King Bergelmir," I said respectfully. The king began the fantastic tale, and like the ocean that spilled from Ymir's wound, the story flooded the table with silence. Bergelmir required a token of peace from my brothers and me after his story was told. As I scanned my brothers' reactions, they looked like they would kill the Jotun king for disrespecting them at the table.

"The day is long. May I retire early?" I asked to stop my brothers from doing something foolish. Without the three of us united, they would not attack. "Tomorrow, I will gift you, my son Ullr. He is a giant boy, even from birth, and he can be raised in Jotunheim as one of your own. Consider this as a gesture of peace, King Bergelmir."

"Not drinking too much, I see, Odin. No one will think you rude if you go to bed early. I will have your son raised by my son, Hymir. He is a great king in the forest of ogres by the sea. And we shall have peace." Vili wished to stay at the table and enjoy the feast and mead, so before I retired, I said to him, "the herd knows when it is time to go home. Only the glutton remains unaware of their limits."

The following day, I left for three days and returned with the bear cub, who began to take human form as I reached the encampment. "You shall return to me, my son. You are destined for a great many accomplishments, and when you are ready, you shall have glory," I said to Ullr, regretfully handing him over to Hymir. As we retired to bed inside the Jotun encampment, our beds were not empty. Vili's boasting never done him any favours. He began to stutter and mumble at the table. Only for his foolishness to return the more mead, he drank. Ve brought laughter to the table, so he was gifted a Jotun maiden to bed that night. I was also gifted a different Jotun maiden. She was a beautiful and strong Jotun lady. Gridr was her name, and she was not so eager to sleep with me. As I lay next to her discussing her hopes and aspirations, I filled her ears with sweet nothings and gently touched her soft skin. The mystic belt around her waist was interesting to me as it loosened. She called it Megingjord, and it would not be the last I would see such a belt. That was when I learned the difference between being grateful and having expectations. I was thankful for the hard days gone, a challenge completed, the slippery ice I had crossed, a drink shared and a lover's embrace.

The night was exhausting, but the sleep that came after was needed. I couldn't help but to hear the familiar chanting of before on the air as I began to drift into slumber. The next day, my brothers and I left Jotunheim to create our own home. The journey was long, and the seas were vast, but we eventually made land. We stepped onto the shore with the nine wave maidens climbing onto land to only be dragged back by Ran, the queen of Vanaheim.

Ymir's skull created the light blue sky with his brains creating the clouds. Suddenly, my brothers discovered two logs that drifted onto the sand. One was from a great ash tree. This tree was helpful in the manufacturing of bows and hunting equipment. The other was from a sturdy elm tree. This wood is most beneficial in building great halls for feasting and celebration. "How about we make something great?" I suggested to my brothers. "How about we create beings to worship us. They will give us allies against the Jotun forces as our peace treaty hangs in a fragile balance. The trolls, ogres and giants are not to be trusted." We all agreed, and we made them similar to our image.

It is wise to do things when they are in your favour. Wonder when the mind is calm. Find support for the dark times ahead. Travel the mind swiftly, remain protected from others and keep your wit sharp. Ve created their shapes. He was the reason they could see, smell and hear, as Ve's senses were so intense, he could listen to the faintest of sounds floating across the winds. Vili granted them intelligence, a fire that would give them the ability to create and destroy their lands. But it was I that gave them life with the breath of inspiration. This would allow them to create greatness and great terror in the world. You can't appreciate the great in this new world if you do not have the capability of catastrophe.

We created man and woman out of ash and elm tree. Their names were simple, named after the trees they originated from, Askr and Embla, and they would populate the realm we had discovered. We found more significant than the usual maggots crawling around. They gnawed at the rotting flesh that remained of Ymir and this gave me an idea. Given a somewhat human form, my brothers and I created the elves. Elves were a collective term, as the species were as diverse as the Jotuns. The dwarves, gnomes, goblins and even the beautiful elves. Next time you see a garden gnome, the house had better take care of its place. The gnomes can protect your dwelling from curses and spirits, but if mistreated, they can become very twisted and cause problems for the family household. The dwarves were great smiths and builders of things imbued with great magics. Vili created the dark elves. These goblins were more suited to the darkness in forests with low sunlight. At night, they would stretch their wings and seek out food. Primarily fruits and nuts from nearby plantations, but those with the taste for blood became very sinister.

The elves and fairies I claimed as my own, as they would supply Asgard with soldiers and warriors. I would claim them under a different name. The sons of Ivaldi would help protect the realms from war. They were beautiful and noble, and their love of gold and silver would create weapons of the purest kind. Their ability to weave clothes using precious metals was astounding. They could make the metal grow like grass in the meadows. It was most impressive.

The dwarves were put to work early; they created the barrier between Jotunheim and Midgard using Ymir's eyebrows. The dwarves used Ymir's tongue to build something magnificent. Colourful, long and rigid bridge that could appear and disappear at our will. It would be called the Bifrost, a rainbow bridge that would become the connection between Asgard and Midgard. We created the halls of Asgard with beams of elm and our seats from stone from Ymir's teeth. They were large and their capacities were great, but each night, we would feast using my great hall. We would share stories and discuss our objectives as leaders of the lands we govern.

# Building the Village

Asgard would be the realm of the Aesir gods. All who were helpful to the tribe were accepted here. Not as bright as the adjacent city of Alfheim. The elves had buildings of gold, roads pathed with yellow bricks, and the rivers shimmered with silver like the stars in the night sky. They existed deep in the heart of the now Amazonian rainforest, living free amongst all kinds of colourful animals. The lands of Alfheim would be called home to fairies, nymphs and elves and they would coexist in a city of gold.

The wise know that riches do not determine your worth. Another's wealth does not reflect your value in life.

Svartalfheim was a realm of industry full of forges and smouldering iron. These were the lands created by rock, iron and timber that harboured the dark elves. These dwarves and goblins harnessed the liquid fires deep within volcanic mountains to create weapons and items of extraordinary ability. Their furnaces were continuously pumping, as there was always something to make. They were hardy little dwarves, valuing strength and hard work over the more refined, more precious metals.

Asgard was a realm amongst the clouds, the perfect balance of both beauty and industry. The realm of the gods contained halls of wood and steel.

The first of the many halls was mine. Valhöll wasn't much at first, a corrugated roof with two goats. You are a master at your home. Even if you have little, that is better than begging. You don't require much in life, just enough to not plead for meat at each meal.

After each battle on Midgard, the Valkyrie would choose the slain to join my hall. Each of the glorious dead would bring a shield and soon, my hall would become the great hall of legend. Even I am not high enough to refuse a gift for a gift. Accepting would not bring me sorrow or anger.

It would have many rooms, and these rooms were filled with the worthy dead from Midgard. If I saw them and could learn from their tales of battle and struggle, they would feast and fight every day to earn their place in the hall. Friendship is the greatest of gifts—mutual giving and receiving to keep life going well. I'd train them for Ragnarök, and they would stand shoulder to shoulder on the field ready for battle. They will stand with the gods when facing our enemies.

The Einherjar are the greatest of warriors collected over the years that have passed; the greatest accumulated over the millennia forged in the furnace of battle and war. My throne, Hlidskjalf, would sit at the highest point of my hall. It was a throne-like no other: a seat where I could view everything from the Jotun forces gathered, the people of Midgard's growth and even beneath the ocean's surface.

Sitting upon my throne I peered beneath the glassy surface of the tranquil seas and there *she was*, in the underwater realm of Vanaheim. She was as beautiful as ever. Jord was at what looked like her brother, Njord's side. Neither looked pleased about it, but as I later learned their parents wished they would create a pure-blooded heir to the throne and looked like they were discussing such matters.

I couldn't help admiring her beauty. She had my heart and sparked the curiosity in my mind. "Why did she deny me her warm embrace? I must win her heart." I thought to myself.

My brothers would continue the construction of Asgard as I departed into the ocean depths. There was an island in Midgard, a small and secret island, with a cave that would provide entrance to Vanaheim. I had the power of birds, so I transformed into a penguin to allow me underwater flight and access to the realm.

Vanaheim was so beautiful with lovely forests and beautiful green as far as the eyes could see, it was like Atlantis of Greek myth. The coral illuminated the city in an air pocket beneath the watery depths.

Aegir and Ran sat on their thrones ruling the best way they saw fit. The warriors were shield maidens and it appeared that there were only two males that existed in the entire society. Njord and Aegir, noble and robust, had the abilities to fly through the water, but also walk in human form on land.

The women there were beautiful, strong and powerful like the Amazonian goddess warriors. It was a utopia full of magic and wonder, however, each child born was feminine and this would infuriate King Aegir. Njord was solely responsible for creating the population and his lack of male heirs left his father disappointed.

After learning what I could visually and eavesdropping, I infiltrated the fortress of my love. Keeping out of sight, I waited for the time when she was alone. "Jord," I whispered faintly enough so she alone could hear it. She couldn't help but smile.

"You came to rescue me?" She asked as she wrapped her arms around me.

"Not yet, my Laufey," I responded regretfully. "I am devising a plan to set you free from your current situation." Her smile dropped from her face slightly with the hope of freedom dwindling. "My love, why did you allow my brothers the pleasures of your embrace and deny me?" I asked curiously, charmed with her beauty.

"How can you appreciate my embrace if I am your first? I gave you Sif to enjoy so that you can appreciate me when the time comes." She leaned over and whispered into my ear, "Tonight is the time."

That night we took each other. It was a consummation like no other. The clouds above rushed through the skies and the earth below shook. Combining the clouds with the land, flashes of light and both earth and the sky trembled as we battled playfully. I heard her utter the magical incantations between the moans and thrusts. The following day came, and the union was known to everyone in all the eight realms.

The next day she gave birth to a huge boy. "His name is Thor. Stronger than both of us, he is a worthy son of leadership," she said, exhausted from the night's activities. "You must take him and hide him from my parents," she instructed. "He will not be allowed his freedom and he will suffer the punishment that my brother currently endures if you do not."

"I will free you, my Laufey," I said, grabbing the child. "You have my oath."

I left for Jotunheim in an attempt to keep Thor from a terrible fate. The journey was long, but I had to be quick. I transformed back into a penguin and entered the waters of Vanaheim swimming as hard and fast as I could through the schools of fish, but something was in pursuit. I turned back for an instant to see a dark silhouette with rows of razor-sharp teeth, swimming in quick hunt. Beyond the teeth, there were eyes as black as Ginnungagap. I was desperately trying to evade the jaws of Ran, narrowly escaping death. I ducked and weaved, changing direction swiftly while I soared through the water like a falcon. She began to tire as I made it to shore with haste.

After scrambling onto land in Midgard, I climbed onto my boat. I began to row hard, and every now and then, I could see Ran's fin following in the vast ocean. The very threat of her caused me to quicken my pace. As I passed the great cliffs that were once Ymir's eyebrows, I could see she seized her attempts on my life. I could finally slow my pace as I sailed into the depths of Jotunheim to seek protection for my son.

Some time had passed since Bergelmir was on the throne. His eldest son claimed the right to rule. He was a resentful king full of spite towards our actions on Ymir. "Ah, little Aesir, what do you want? Haven't my people suffered enough at you and your brothers' hands?" The Jotun ogre scowled.

"Great king, I knew your father and he was an honourable Jotun. I ask you to provide my son refuge as a gesture of peace," I pleaded. The king paused as a sinister smile came over his face.

"I will do this for you, Odin. In return you must take your brother's son. Honir, the fool. He is entertaining for a time, but the idiot becomes annoying after a while," he stated as his grin became a smile. "I will look after your boy personally but know this, Odin. He will suffer a great torment and torture for your actions on Ymir." I couldn't react even though every ounce of me wanted to run him through with my spear. Asgard could not have war with both Jotunheim and Vanaheim. I regretfully left with Honir by my side. He looked noble like a king, but when he spoke, it was the words of a fool.

As we rowed past the eyebrows of Ymir, we were confronted with sword-like teeth and eyes as black as darkest depths of the ocean. A shark emerged from the surface, taking female form. "Odin, is this the boy you had with Jord?" Ran snarled, eager to take us to the depths. "No, beautiful queen. This boy is my brother's child. He is Honir, a hardy god born of Ve and a Jotun from Jotunheim," I informed her while remaining humble and respectful of her power.

"Lucky for you, Odin, because if I catch your boy on the water, I will take him and he will become a servant of Aegir," She warned before retreating beneath the surface. Now understanding why Ran was so adamant to pursue us, we rowed off toward Midgard with a little less haste.

As we travelled the lands of Midgard, we would stop at homes but only when we needed rest. The families would gift a warm meal in exchange for a tale or two. We travelled under the guise of weary, old wanderers to not appear deserving of help or aid. I didn't want fame or respect from these people. I just wanted them to live in peace, but any that did not host us in such a way, would come across some knowledge about an unfaithful wife or a plague upon their life.

As we finally approached the Bifrost, I called my brother Ve. "Open the Bifrost!" And with a flash of light engulfing both of us, we travelled to the clouds.

Upon our arrival, we were greeted by my brother, who wrapped his arms around me and asked about my companion. I reminded him of the time spent in Jotunheim. As he laughed and joked, he slowly recalled his pastimes with the Jotun maiden, and I watched as his smile fell from his face. He then became quiet and acknowledged my honourable return.

After the small reunion with Ve, we left my brother's home behind in Himinbjorg and marched towards the throne. Vili sat high and mighty on it while looking down at all the domains. Kingship did not suit him at all. He sat behind the mighty table that could seat eight hundred men or women. It was carved from solid wood, unbreakable even from the mightiest blow, and each warrior would have to earn their seat. I hammered my fist into the table, demanding the right to rule. "I have done more to keep the peace than you have, brother. I gave both life and peace to the realms." He sat there and smirking, belittling my accomplishments.

"I am the eldest and it is my birthright," Vili replied, puffing his chest out.

"Let's put it to a vote then, brother," I suggested confidently. "Let the three sons of Bor decide who should lead." Vili agreed ignorantly, clueless of the child I returned.

"Fetch Ve so we can get this over with, little brother," Vili instructed from his high seat.

I returned with Ve by my side. "Who do you support in leadership, brother? Young Odin or me?" Asked Vili. Ve's face remained unchanged while deciding.

"Odin has accomplished much in these lands. He returned my son to me from Jotunheim," Ve announced.

Vili's expression changed into desperation. "But brother, are you forgetting our children that share similar nature?" He asked, hoping to bond and persuade.

"The wolves that sit by the throne. They are loyal but troublesome beasts. They eat and devour all the meat and sometimes the bone. They must be fed continually to ensure their allegiance to the throne. Our brother Odin can assure they will be kept sustained, unlike what you are able to guarantee for their survival," Ve replied.

"There you have it, brother. I am the leader of the Aesir tribe," I confirmed respectfully. Vili glared through me with envy.

"One condition," chorused the brothers.

"Name it as I wish to work together," I replied.

"You must accept Geri and Freki in a blood oath. This oath will tie you three together forever and ensure you will not be responsible for spilling each other's blood. Any of you would be eternally accepted at any table the others attended. Each will be at your side sharing in feast and honour," Vili declared while Ve agreed.

"I swear. Any meal given shall be shared with the wolves until both our appetites are met. I swear I shall not allow his blood to be spilled as he will ensure my blood remains in its veins," I said while taking the tip of my spear to my finger, testing the sharpness.

I instructed them to come closer as I sliced my hands and both their tongues. I placed each hand upon each of the wolves' tongues. That day, the blood oaths were taken. They became bound to me, much closer than my brothers. Those that share in the spilling of blood are far more bonded than those that share in the spilling of water.

I would attempt to lead, not simply instruct, and there was much to learn about all the eight realms. A great leader doesn't sit back and watch the world go by from the throne. He gets involved in experiencing the hardships that lesser men have. How can you fix a problem if you do not fully understand it through ordeals? It is impossible to comprehend situations while sitting in comfort. Allowing others to do your work will not provide much wisdom. However, being involved with the planning and getting encompassed in the very things you wish to fix provides more valuable lessons.

# A Father's Tears

For a time, there was peace in the eight realms. Elves, Vanir, Aesir and even the Jotun lived in peace to my regret. All flourished under my leadership. They existed in harmony, but I was plagued by my actions regarding Thor. I walked to my throne to assess my boys' living situations in Jotunheim. There was nothing that I wanted more than to have them by my side. I looked to the lands of the Jotuns, and I could see Ullr fishing with Hymir. He was learning patience and resilience from his foster father. I couldn't have been prouder watching as they pulled whales from the sea. Seeing a somewhat positive upbringing made me reluctant to alter my gaze towards Thor.

He endured torture and ridicule by that terrible Jotun king. He was not allowed to open his mouth unless to eat the scraps they left him. To do anything not to the Jotun's liking, he would have to withstand punishment, or even worse, a beating. My tears rolled down both cheeks while I kept quiet. I saw the strength of my boy develop and grow far beyond that of my own. Each time he was struck down, every time he was mistreated, he pent it up. A great storm brewed inside Thor like lightning in a bottle, but every bottle has its limits.

I stood up from the throne as an elf guard entered. "Odin, we have a visitor," he said. At the same time, my eyes were on my boys, I had missed someone's approach to Asgard. "Who is it?" I asked as it was the first time, we had visitors.

"A sorceress from Vanaheim, my king. She brings maidens and wishes to speak with you." I knew how deadly those warrior maidens could be, even if they were only a fraction of Rans power. "Bring her in," I was curious to the reasoning behind her travels so far from home.

I sat up straight on my throne with Geri and Freki by my side. When she entered, the wolves began a low growl. Their eyes fixed on her movements with mouths salivating. "Who are you? What news do you bring from Vanaheim?" I asked, immediately cautious of an attempt on my life. "Ran knew I had a child with her daughter, so why could they want peace now?" I pondered while assessing the threat.

"Great Odin, I am Gulveig. I am handmaiden to Jord, and I bring many a beautiful maiden to your kingdom. I bring the great magic of Seidr to teach your warriors and people." I already learned this magic but didn't want to appear greedy and selfish to the rest of my kingdom. Her beauty intoxicated me long enough for my wolves to slip my control. They rushed Gulveig, but she was ready. This mistress of magical abilities, a Völva, and she manipulated Seidr like I hadn't seen before.

The wind rushed in behind her, stopping the wolves in their tracks. Words echoed around the room and her eyes burned with gold. The wolves crouched low trying to use their claws to keep their footing, but unfortunately, it was to no avail. Their bodies slammed against the wall, and something strange happened. The two wolves began to merge. Both struggled and whimpered with pain and panic. After a few moments of hurt and howls, someone emerged. It was Loki. At that moment, both Vili and Ve burst through the doors.

"Odin? Is everything ok here?" Ve asked with a hand firmly gripping his sword.

"Where are our children?" Vili asked with such a scowl on his face. I was silent, still in shock by what I observed. He was male but quite feminine in appearance. He had fiery red hair with dark green eyes. He was slender in stature, but he had a strange attractiveness to him. His tongue was both literally and metaphorically forked as one-half truth here could mean deception elsewhere. His demeanor was not unlike a politician today. Half truths appear noble but not to incite panic amongst the people.

"You are looking at them," Loki spoke with a forked tongue and devious smile. Vili was enraged.

"You were supposed to look after my boy, Odin. Now he's, well he's that." Loki's smile dropped as his father's words hit his ears.

"Fatherssss," he hissed, "I am still me. Just different."

Ve looked at him and embraced Loki. "You will be my child regardless of Vili's poisonous words."

Vili scolded the entire room. "You are now under Odin's service, creature, you disgusting and unnatural thing."

I stood up and thumped my spear against the ground. "Silence, fool! I have the oath to protect your child. This includes your heinous words!" My voice echoed around the hall, billowing from beneath the earth. It was as if Jord herself gave me the voice to defend her child. Vili turned his back on Loki and me. As he left, I turned to Gulveig. "You brought powerful magic and beautifully strong women to Asgard. For that reason, you are welcome to celebrate and feast amongst the Aesir. Teach them this magic. On the third day, you will return to Vanaheim with our allegiance. Tell Aegir and Ran…"

"Forgive me, king," she interrupted, "it is Jord and Njord who have assumed the throne. Aegir and Ran have retired to the depths. They desire respect for their rule over the realm of Vanaheim." I approved as now my love sat on the throne.

"Let us begin the three days of celebration!" I declared as we retired to Valhöll to begin the festivities for peace.

# The Burning of Gulveig

We celebrated loud and proud with the shield maidens from Vanaheim. Gulveig sat next to me while we shared stories, food and mead. "Please tell me of the red-haired queen," I asked Gulveig, intoxicated as my thoughts drifted to our night together.

"She rules next to her brother in hopes of providing the king a pure-blooded heir," she replied as another across the table drew her gaze. She attempted to gain the attention of the newly created Loki. It appeared she had lustful thoughts and desires of her own.

Loki subtly glanced across at Gulveig with his crafty green eyes and plans for the maiden. "May I leave, Odin? I wissshhh to retire early tonight." Loki respectfully asked.

"No one will judge you poorly if you go to bed early," I said profoundly. A few moments after Loki's departure, I noticed the seat at my side was vacant. My view was focused on another, that I never noticed Gulveig had slipped away. I spoke to Sif for a time with humble apologies. "Sif, what had occurred is not what I intended," I said as my head hung in shame. She looked up at me with smiling eyes. I was taken back by the reaction. Her words fell on my ears, providing comfort from embarrassment.

"King, you were outwitted by a woman far superior in magic than you. I'm sure she did what she did for a reason," Sif reassured softly. I felt a great weight lift from my burdened conscience and returned to the celebrations.

The next day Gulveig appeared different. She was not the intimidating Völva she once was but was more reserved. At breakfast, she flinched, seemed edgy and wouldn't reply to any of my concerns. When Loki entered proudly in his new form, I noticed Gulveig lowering her head. "How was your night, Loki?" I asked curiously.

"It wasss educational, all father," he replied subtly towards Gulveig. I suspected no good but was sure the Völva would have advised me of any wrongs she was subjected to. We returned to eating the breakfast feast before I gave fair maiden a tour of Asgard.

Later that night, Loki devoured the food at the speed of two wolves. Again, he slipped away, and again Gulveig was nowhere to be seen. I searched the castle, only to find there was no trace of them. I returned to the festivities in hopes either would return, and noticed there was a subtle sound in the air. This time it was not a female voice but a sinister hiss that echoed on the faint night breeze. I knew what was going on now, and I'd have to reign in my wolves.

The following day Gulveig was the shell of a woman she once was, bruised and scratched as if tooth and claw had torn the very spirit, she once possessed from within her. "Are you ok, fair maiden?" I asked sensitively.

"I'm fine," she replied softly. The wise never fully trust the words of another; look deeper as words mask something more. Emotions can run high while keeping the illusion of peace when exhausted or mistreated by another.

"Loki!" I yelled, making the skies grumble with my booming voice. "A young tree dies when exposed to the elements. Same as a person without love. Why should they live long, Loki? This must stop, or the peace between Asgard and Vanaheim will not last." Loki looked down to avoid eye contact.

"Yesss sssire," he hissed quietly under his breath.

"Apologies, Gulveig, I was unaware of your treatment at the hands of Loki Laufeyson." Her eyes widened with shock. She knew her queen had gone by that name at one point and that Njord wouldn't be happy if he found out this information.

"It's ok, Odin," she shuttered. This apparent disrespect ignited a fire in his eyes.

It was the last night of feasting in the celebration of peace. It was odd that Loki never attended, but the feasting continued regardless. All shared celebration and happiness. "It's probably for the best he isn't here," Gulveig mentioned in my ear.

"Let's not talk about it. There is much mead to be shared," I declared while raising my drinking horn. The night was getting late, meaning it was time for the party to disperse.

Gulveig returned to her room, relieved that she didn't have to deal with Loki's Seidr magic on her. She locked the door, and as she lay on the bed, she felt malicious eyes upon her naked body. Loki appeared from the shadows. "You think of me as nothing more than a wild beast? I can show you the same disrespect with my lack of care for you and your children." Gulveig looked into his green eyes, paralysed with fear. She closed her eyes until it was over. It didn't take long before Loki uttered the words.

"I now have three of your seeds in me," she said softly. "Will you at least hand fast yourself to me?" Gulveig asked. Loki looked down at her body with an elevated ego and replied with words that would feel like a spear to her heart. She was burned three times by Loki's use of the very magic she brought. Her heart ached as if it was speared through with his hurtful words regarding his care for his children. Her appearance transformed into something quite monstrous. Before morning light, she escaped Asgard under cover of darkness. "You will regret this, mark my words. I will curse you and the Aesir for accepting such a twisted creature into their ranks."

# No Peace Without War

When I woke in the morning, I searched high and low for Gulveig. I soared across Asgard, looking for a trace of her, but it was as if she had never existed at all. Loki strolled in with a smug grin on his face.

"Perhaps she went home, Odin," he said, thinking that would ease my concern.

"Loki, it is best to be half wise, not over cunning or clever. Only know what you need. A greed for knowledge or power never brings happiness," I replied to the jester.

"Use your throne, all father, if you are concerned. Perhapsss we can convince her to leave on good terms," Loki suggested.

"Good idea, boy," I said to him because the price of praise is low. I knew what he had done. He went directly against my instructions.

I sat on Hlidskjalf, scanning the nearby surroundings in desperation. It wasn't long before I concluded that she had run off and made it to Vanaheim. I looked towards the city and saw that she was informing Njord of something serious based on her body language and facial expressions. She was covered in a long, ominous cloak that hung over her twisted body. Once a beautiful maiden was now twisted into a dark witch hag.

I had great eyes, but the hearing went to Ve. There was no mistake. I could see Njord was angered as the seas began to rise and claim the land that my brothers and I made with Jord's rescue. I would call for council with my brothers to seek their recommendations.

"Needing help already, brother?" Vili mocked.

"Silence Vili, a good king seeks input from equals before finalising his decisions. What do you require of us, Odin?" Ve asked respectfully after scalding Vili.

"Brothers, what would you have me do? I suspect Njord now knows of Loki's origins. Thanks to our guest, your child could cause the greatest war that will leave the realms and their inhabitants in shatters. My oath bounds me to his protection, but I will have to admit that his death would make things easier for the world."

"You made the oath, little brother. Now you keep it. You're smart. You can find some way to win the war," Vili said condescendingly.

"Meet with Njord, brother. Hear his demands and negotiate another attempt at peace," Ve suggested.

"That's it then. The decision has been made. I will seek out wiser counsel from Mimir in Jotunheim before I attempt peace with king Njord."

"I will accompany you, brother, for your protection, of course," volunteered Vili.

"You can't expect to be met with peace with a show of power. He who travels widely needs his wits about him. The stupid should stay at home. The ignorant man is often laughed at when he sits at meat with the sage," I said as this was my journey to endure alone.

Vili turned his back on me regardless of the wise words, but I had more pressing concerns on my mind. I left Asgard immediately with little provisions on the long, harrowing journey over the treacherous mountains of Jotunheim. The climb was steep, and the winds made it more challenging. Still I pressed on, as Mimir's guidance was required and I needed to reach him as swiftly as I could. Eventually, I broke through the veil to Jotunheim, but the journey was longer still over the mountains of bones and the teeth of Ymir until I reached Mimir's well.

"Dear nephew, what brings you here, I wonder," Mimir smugly asked like he didn't already know.

"Uncle, I seek your wise counsel. What should I do?" Mimir smiled and told me in the most cryptic of ways.

"King of the gods, I know what you'll do. Until now, you've sacrificed for peace, but now comes another path. Sometimes the path is not the one that provides the least resistance. The top of a mountain has many paths and if you choose one, sometimes doubling back is impossible. The choices you have made previously have led you here, accept them and move forward. Bring me Honir, and I will attempt to make a leader of him." I left puzzled by his cryptic advice. He always said just enough to leave me thinking, but my mind found the pleasures in deciphering his riddles.

The journey back was long and hard, but by the time I had reached Asgard, Ve informed me of visitors from Vanaheim. I hurried as quickly as I could to meet the king and queen of the Vanir gods.

"About time you showed up," Njord huffed.

"Forgive me, Njord, I had to learn of how I can fix such wrongs," I replied while Jord drew my gaze. "My lady," I acknowledged her presence with the utmost respect.

"Careful with your eyes, Odin. They reveal too much of your intentions for my sister."

"Ah yes, dear Njord, what would you have me do?" I responded.

"I want the head of that creature that took Gulveig's beauty from her. I know it is a child of my sister and your brothers, Odin. I want its head!" I could see the oceans rise with Njord's temper.

"I have an oath of protection with Loki, and I always keep my oaths," I said, looking him directly in the eyes. "There must be something else, anything else?" I asked but already knew the answer. I could see Njord's temper peaking and turned from him with my spear in hand.

"How dare you turn your back to me, Aesir king," Njord scolded. I turned to look at my beloved Jord in her green eyes as her red hair flowed to her shoulders. I gave her an intense stare while an impossible choice weighed down my heart. I decided to walk toward the balcony of my throne room. Turning to the side, I prepared to launch my spear. It took flight and soared fast and high amongst the clouds. Gliding like a bird through the air, it spotted its prey. It dove down, moving at such a speed that the keenest of eyes struggle to make out its shape. Down it went and pierced the surface of the great sea, still not slowed by the resistance in the water, only to reach the final destination in Vanaheim.

"War it is then," Njord huffed, upset with his lack of persuasion and intimidation.

"It is. Go home now, king of the Vanir. I will not spill your blood today. We will have our war in the morning," I warned him. "Apologies, my lady. I wish there were another way," I said to Jord as she left with her brother.

She turned around and looked me in my eyes, "I am not your lady, Odin, not yet." Always puzzling me with cryptic words and sentences. It was like she cast a spell of madness while I scrambled to find their meaning.

# The Wandering Dead

So it began, the Great War, the first war and the most devastating to the eight realms. Many fell from all lands. Humans, Jotun and even animals perished at the devastation the war brought. With the clashing of swords against shields, the screams of the dying falling never to rise again, the Valkyrie were extremely busy in those years. This carnage continued for decades with no clear winner in sight. The destruction was too much to bear, and after all my brothers and I created, there wouldn't be anything left to rule.

The halls in Asgard were filling up with the dead. Each gallery was reaching its capacity. The dead would have nowhere to rest if the war continued and the world of the living would suffer if I did not find a solution. I withdrew the forces of Asgard and Alfheim back to their respective homes, it was time to put an end to this. An endless war would not provide much glory of life if they had to suffer so much death.

Those that had unfinished business would rise again. Decayed and rotten, they moved slowly towards those they felt wronged by in life. It was unfortunate for those who crossed them while they wandered their paths at night. They had pale lifeless eyes, filled with regrets and blind to their lessons in death. They groaned with each step taken in the darkest of nights, they were hungry to sustain themselves on the living.

My journey began through the lands of Midgard. I noticed that some villagers were under stress. The undead tortured their village and claimed many lives. It was a cold wintery night with blizzards that could freeze your bones. On my journey I noticed a warm, flickering flame appearing through the window of a logwood cabin that was like a beacon of hope. As I struggled up to the entrance, weary from braving the elements, I raised my hand to knock on the door. Not too much to cause a panic, just enough to know someone was waiting, three purposeful knocks on the door.

"If you are a Draugr, go away, undead wanderer!" Warned the lonely old homeowner. He came up to his locked door and slid open the peephole. Upon seeing I was not one of the undead, he opened the door immediately and invited me in quickly securing us within.

"All hail the givers! A guest has come, and I am in no rush to the fire, out of respect to my honourable host," I said, humbled by his welcome.

"Fire is needed for those that venture in the cold. Food and clothing to those that have travelled far," the man replied wisely. Such words made me an honoured guest with a man who had less than I did.
"Water too, so he may wash before eating. A hand cloth, too, so he may dry his hands with more than the fire. Welcome, dear friend. What is your name?" He asked courteously.

"Ivaldi the wanderer," I replied, then returned to silence.

"I apologise. I don't have much in terms of food, but how did you manage to avoid the Draugr?" He asked in awe.

"No apologies needed, good host. I have already eaten a ham with a friend that had two. What are Draugr?" I replied, clueless and curious for more information.

"The Draugr are the dead people with unfinished business. They appear to be increasing in number and frequency of attack. I'm surprised you haven't come across them," the man said while seeming puzzled.

I had heard enough to work out the reasons behind such creatures. Even the halls of Asgard had their limits and if the dead had nowhere to go, they would become Draugr to plague the land of the living. Undead warriors are pretty hard to kill, but a flame seems to keep them away. "Wits are needed for those that travel far. The dumb should stay at home. The quiet will be laughed at if they don't say much when seated with wise men," I thought to myself. "I have travelled from distant lands gracious host but have longer yet to travel. I came over mountains and braced the blizzards. I have yet to cross the ocean and make it to fix the devastation I have caused."

"Such a noble quest for any man to carry out, Ivaldi," he replied. "Let us fill your belly enough for your journey wise wanderer while you tell me your tales of adventure."

I never revealed enough that he'd be aware of my true identity and feel the need to give me all; that wasn't my desire. That night I gained a friend, the greatest gift of all. Mutual giving and receiving to ensure all keeps going well. I retired early to bed as much of the journey still lay ahead.

The next day I rose before the sun and noticed the fire was dwindling. The gracious host had fallen asleep before feeding the fire. I could hear the groans of the undead Draugr as they appeared to be getting closer as the flames died. I hurried to grab a bottle of mead and a piece of wood from the fireplace when they burst through the doors and rushed towards the slumbering man. I would not let them have their pray, and with a mouth full of mead and a stick that still had an ember on it, I used a dragon's breath. It consumed the Draugr and engulfed them in flame, as they retreated from the house. They would never return to bother the man again.

"Bu..bu, but how?" He asked, stumbling over his words.

"Wits my host. The flame kept them away out of fear, and now they remain dead. Apologies, but I must go," I respectfully informed him.

"My name is Hans, old wanderer, and you will always be welcome in my home if you need a bed and a meal."

"if you have much, you should always extend your table to those that don't," I said, smiling faintly. I gave a wink to thank you as I left to continue my journey.

# A Show of Strength

My journey led up the mountainous terrain that was once Ymir's bones. The frost and bitter winds tried their best to disrupt my attempts to gain peace. Blistering cyclones attempted to blow me down the mountain while the snow pelted me in the face like shards of glass. Still, I marched on with purpose. Each step was a battle of resilience. Through Jotunheim's brutal domain, I wandered cloaked as an old man. The climb down was more complicated, with each step causing rock and stone to crumble and dislodge themselves beneath my footing. Stone cascaded down the mountain like an avalanche over my dreams of peace, crumbling before me. Once I had reached the bottom, the journey to my uncles began.

The journey was long, but my steps were quick. When my journey culminated at Mimir's well, I sighed with relief. Honir was there attempting to learn from Mimir's wisdom. I thought it was an odd request at first, but my uncle knew more than I did. "Odin, my favourite student. Have you come to take Honir to Vanaheim?" he asked.

"Uncle, you are a trustworthy friend. I do wish well for you, honestly. I bring gifts and share our stories, but your journey is not here. I require your aid for peace with Vanaheim" I replied. I looked at my uncle's face as it seemed to show concern.

We retired out of reach of Honir's ears. "He looks the part nephew, but a wise leader he is not," Mimir hung his head in failure.

"Small is the minds of many, uncle. Not all are equal in wisdom. People are only half wise in different topics. Perhaps I have an idea," I said ominously.

"I have done enough, nephew. I wish to rest," he claimed.

"Those that rely on old accomplishments will not find support in the future. You can accompany him as an advisor. That would ensure Honir's leadership decisions were respected in replacing Njord's rule. It is the only way this will work. The realms are in chaos as it is now," I instructed my wise uncle. He reluctantly agreed without uttering a word. It was like he was expecting the worse and knew it was coming.

The three of us left the safety of Mimir's home to venture out to journey towards Vanaheim. Before long, we were back amongst the treacherous waves that rocked the boat violently. The spray of the sea created a mist so thick that we could barely see beyond the edge of the ship. Still, we harnessed the gales to guide our boat to the entrance of the underwater realm. The closer we came to the island that provided entry, the more dangers. There were sharks eager to feast on our bodies. They were chomping and snapping at each other, fighting for dominance before their feast was provided. Trying to navigate the ship into the harbour safely proved quite challenging. We had to predict the unnatural currents while being almost submerged by the giant waves. Mimir tied the boat to the dock, consumed with thoughts of what will happen in the future. "No man can know his future. Rest easy, uncle," I said, hoping he'd relax and become more comfortable with the trade.

Silence fell on the lands of Vanaheim. It was eerie and quiet. The winds whispered, sending shudders up my back. The corals provided light within the realm beneath the sea weren't as luminescent as before. Vanaheim was dark and empty without a glimmer of hope. Honir's ears were far more sensitive than mine and he heard the familiar groans of the undead. It was apparent that everyone had their encounters with the wandering dead, even the gods. The Draugr had reached this place.

As we approached Njord's hall, we used fire to deter the beasts' attacks, when we were surrounded by darkness and the undead. I waved the torch toward them to warn them off. They were hungry and wretched creatures. They parted as soon as the light from the flame got close to them, clearing a path to the entrance.

"Njord!!! Open your gates!!! I have come with soup and water!" I yelled echoing through the chasm of the underwater kingdom. The clunking and creaking of the old doors as they opened gave me hope. I lit the fire as soon as I entered, which kept the Draugr away. "This war has gone on long enough, Njord. The undead rise and not much will be left for the living. Even the glorious Vanaheim has been left gloomy and hopeless," I told the king.

"We are hungry, Odin. Our supplies have gotten scarce, and we are tired from keeping our walls barricaded," Njord said, exhausted from the battles he faced over the years. "Many warriors have fallen, but the ranks of the undead rise with each warrior that dies," he said.

"Say no more," I told him as I reached into my bag, pulling out all that was needed to brew a hearty soup and enough bread to feed all in Vanaheim. Often a little thing will win your favour. I won friends that day with just half a loaf of bread and a cauldron of soup.

We sat down and broke bread. The conversation happened after our meal, and it was a long one. "If you come back to Asgard, we can unite the tribes and become stronger. Peace in Yggdrasil is the most important thing to me," I said, trying to convince the king of Vanaheim.

"I am to give up my title and position to serve you elevated gods of Asgard? Pfft, you must think me a fool," Njord replied in disgust.

"No king, you would serve on the council as my equal. No god will be elevated above another. We are all equals on the council. We will work together for the good of all: Jotun kind, elf kind, humankind. We have a duty and responsibility to ensure chaos doesn't prevail," I reassured Njord quickly. "Leadership is not for those that wish to live above another but those that wish to work together for better outcomes for all," I said profoundly.

"Who will rule Vanaheim in my absence?" Asked Njord.

"Well, my friend, here is my nephew Honir. He is a strong god who, with his trusted teacher and adviser Mimir, will be good in battle. You can rest assured that Vanaheim will be in good hands."

"Before I agree, what do you wish in return, Odin?" Njord quizzed me, suspicious of my desires.

"Peace and the hand of your sister, my good friend," I said respectfully.

"My sister needs to give me an heir before I agree to that," Njord huffed.

"Go to bed tonight, my friend, and in the morning, your heir will be born. I have travelled widely and learned much magic to ensure it."

That night we all retired to the sleep chambers with the fire glowing brightly to keep the Draugr away. With the incantations I chanted on the night breeze, the peace treaty was one step closer to being fulfilled.

They had a boy that night and it brought happiness to Njord and Vanaheim. It would be Freyr Njordson that would be the light to fight the darkness in the god realms. Later that night, unknown to everyone else, I also had a visitor. My beloved Jord visited. We both cast the magic of Seidr, and our two boys were the result. These boys were unlike any of the god children, they would experience life first as mortals creating their own legend. One child was gifted to a wealthy family and raised to be a king. His name was Hödr in the language of the gods. The other to Hans, the wise old man I met in Midgard so long ago. He would be raised to understand humility and was called Agnar, but his true name was Baldur. These boys would live amongst the people of Midgard hidden from Njord and the other gods, their fates intertwined with one another. They would not know of their lineage and not know their actual names until they ascended to Asgard. We would meet again in the future, but much still had to be completed.

# The Rise of Donar

I departed after dropping off my sons in Midgard. Baldur and Hödr would grow up in different situations, but both would cross paths again. I left Midgard to find Thor, my second son, as his suffering had lasted long enough. Using Hlidskjalf every day, I could see that his struggles had developed his strength. He was still treated as an inconvenient enslaved person, held down at a lower level than an animal. The Jotun king beat him at a moment's notice for minor things. Even when Thor did everything to the Jotun king's liking, he would find another reason to raise his hand against my boy. My heart had to endure my son's torture but Thor would rise to a strength greater than even my own despite it all.

The Jotun king would constantly make bitter statements against the gods. Then he would turn to Thor as a physical outlet of his hate. My boy was beaten to his knees and sometimes left in a pool of blood, spit and sweat. For that alone, he always had my respect. He endured many difficulties that developed his strength, resolve and fighting spirit. Thor would be Jotunheim's downfall and my plan all along. I picked the Jotun that would raise my boy even though the king thought he decided. I used the king's resentment and easily manipulated him. His hatred toward me would ensure the survival of Thor. He wished for Thor to suffer, and his death would mean a release of such torments. As a father, you can't fight the battles for your children. You can only endure their struggles and prepare them for what comes next.

While I trekked towards my boy, my all-seeing eyes could view the conspiring plans. The Jotuns planned to dethrone me and the destruction of Asgard. While Thor completed some duties for the foolish Jotun king, he entered where they plotted against his people. "The gods are weak. We should attack now to catch them off guard," one of the trolls on the council suggested. The troll king snatched his cup from Thor before kicking him to the ground.

"Quicker next time, boy, or you will be the first of the gods to die," the Jotun king threatened.

"Eewww, you keep one as a pet?" An ogre asked in disgust.

"No, my hounds receive more than him. He is merely my amusement, a mere toy for me to play with," the king replied. "He will do nothing when his people fall. He will be in chains, watching as we lay waste to his people and toy with the weak people of Midgard." Just then, something stirred as a dark cloud rolled over the land. Like filling a bottle past its limit, the storm within was bound to spill over.

"You will not harm my people," Thor mumbled under his breath.

"What did you say, you mongrel?" he asked, ill-tempered and unhappy mocking all that he heard from the boy. He was quick to find fault in others while remaining blind to his own mistakes.

"You will not harm my people," Thor said a little louder raising his eyes to meet the king. Then, the king raised his hand. Thor caught his fist mid punch. "No!" Thor shouted as the thunder rumbled loudly overhead. He replaced his words with actions in an unavoidable battle. He cracked a smile, almost finding joy in his calling. It was his destiny to control the unruly Jotuns. Why not enjoy it while it is his to hold.

At that moment, the boy went from a quiet slave to a force of unimaginable power. Every ogre, every giant and every troll would know and fear the power of Thor. The king was the first to fall. With a swift blow to the head, he was on the ground. Each hit that followed created a mist of blood that sprayed the entire hall. Every Jotun that charged and tried to subdue Thor was tossed aside quickly. After the king lay unconscious, Thor turned his attention to the others. Each Jotun attempted to fight or flee.

Those that were brave enough to fight had their lives ended brutally. Heads punched clean of their shoulders, hearts torn from chest cavities and limbs ripped out of their sockets. The screams of pain and fear echoed throughout Jotunheim. It was so loud that the blood of the largest giant would turn cold. So cold that their knees would tremble like the teeth of an old man on the snowiest of mountains. All in Jotunheim now understood the price required for threatening the gods. The cost would be their lives.

Shortly after, the clouds of thunder dispersed as Thor's rage-fuelled rampage ended. He was breathing heavily, surrounded by bodies and covered in blood. He left the hall with walls stained with Jotun blood as he stumbled away from his old residence. In the distance, he could make out a shadowy figure at the edge of the woods.

I watched my son struggle towards me, and I raised my spear. My aim was sharp. I threw it hard and fast, giving the spear flight. It was a straight throw, piercing through the air like a bird diving for its prey, anticipating the movements.

Unknown to Thor the Jotun king had his axe raised above his head. Thor was blind to what was occurring behind him. I threw my spear from a great distance, and it flew over his shoulder as he turned. The foolish king fell to his knees and with a mighty thud, he was on his back, never to rise again. "You are talented at this, my boy. The best of lives are attained by gaining experience in that which you enjoy," I said to the little warrior. "The generous and brave live best and are rarely sad for long, boy. The cowardly are afraid of everything, even suspicious of a gift when they receive one. And my boy you are far from cowardly," I said as he panted like an exhausted stag after fighting for its life.

Thor came to the realisation it was an ally in the distance. As his gaze met the falling corpse of the Jotun king with a spear in his chest, he felt relief. He grabbed my spear and plucked it from the corpse's chest. He walked towards me thankful with his eyes drawn to my spear. As corpses lay still, he grabbed what mead horns he could that were still filled with alcohol from the dead Jotun. "Boy, better gear and good sense a traveller can carry. More than the burden of too much drink. Less good than most belief is too much mead. Most know less the more they drink, inevitably becoming a fool," I said looking in his eyes with pride. "Those that have seen and suffered much, know the way of the world. You are now wise enough to know what governs another's actions." He looked at me realising the truth. Everything that had happened, was supposed to. Being a father and a king wasn't without its dilemmas. For the good of the world, you had to endure your child's woes, always hoping for them to make it through becoming stronger on the way.

"I know you're tired, but we have one more stop before we can go home. We must hurry before these corpses begin to move once more," I warned Thor.

"But father I can slay them again," Thor boasted.

"And how do you kill that which is already dead, boy?" As soon as the words left my mouth, I had an idea. "Quick use the fire to burn the dead. We can use their fear against them." We scrambled for torches to burn the dead. "When travelling far, it is better to have a weapon and not need it than to need a weapon and not have one," I said to him before we left for the long journey towards the ironwoods of Jotunheim. I had an old acquaintance to meet again, and a weapon might be needed for protection. Thor reached down for one of the ogre's clubs and began to practice with it.

# Angerboda's Brood

The journey was long over treacherous mountains and rocky paths. My mind wandered, consumed with the thoughts of the Draugr and how to handle those that already existed. With each challenging step taken, my mind was drawn to my brother, Vili. He had power over fire and his sword, Sumarbrandr, gave the wielder a unique ability. The sword, even half unsheathed, would strike fear into an enemy's heart. Most rivals would submit even hearing the blade's name, but on the off chance someone would cross swords with it, a great dance would be had. It was as if the wielder was writing a symphony of blood. The Draugr would be grounded effortlessly, and he could consume the undead with flame, never to rise again.

We approached the dark ironwoods. I got a vision of a being that would be most useful in the control of the ever-rising dead. There was four legs, black fur and sharp teeth. It was only a pup, but our fates were intertwined. Verdandi herself would see to that.

This creature was not alone. My visions would reveal the glistening scales like polished chainmail. Its fangs were dripping with toxic venom. It was a creature that would grow to an intimidating size with flashes of thunder and lightning as the seas raged on.

The third was an innocent little girl. She was beautiful, but as she turned, her face revealed flesh rotten and decayed. Still, she seemed quiet and pleasant. As the vision continued, I saw Draugr by the millions. Each of them treated the girl like royalty, forever in servitude.

We continued through the dark, leafless trees, crooked and twisted like a bony old hag's fingers. These ironwoods were full of unknown dangers ahead, the light barely cracked through the dark clouds above. In the absence of light, darkness prevails. The beautiful bright beams of the sun could not penetrate this wood. There were goblins and creatures of dark nature that crept between the twisted branches. Down the twisted path, we went with only stone and dry dirt beneath our feet. In the centre of the wood, there was a cave even darker than the forest. As we stepped through it, spiderwebs hit our faces. Brushing them away, I noticed they were becoming denser. The sounds of spiders scurrying along the walls filled the damp air of the cave. As we neared our destination in the deepest part of the cave, I turned and whispered to Thor. "Those that have lived unwisely should not be judged, boy. Gulveig has children and worthy works. She was once a beautiful maiden full of good intentions and gifts of knowledge. Her form is due to Loki's use of the magic that created him, and her actions are due to the effects of her brood."

We edged closer to the heart of the cave only to discover the small girl from my visions with an unusual snake coiled around her. Her face did not appear decayed just yet, but the wolf pup by her side had glowing red eyes and teeth bared towards me. It had so much anger, that little wolf that hated me so.

The snake constricted tighter on the young girl causing the life glow to drain from her face. Thor sprinted to help the girl while a monstrous figure descended from the roof behind us.

"Odin," snarled the giant spider maiden. With all eight eyes upon me, she was distracted from Thor. I decided to try my luck to charm her keeping her focussed on me.

"Gulveig, you look as beautiful as ever," I bluffed while trying to appear sincere.

"Gulveig is dead. I am Angerboda now, and your lapdogs caused this," she replied aggressively.

"True, but my eyes can see more than what appears on the surface, fair maiden. You are still beautiful as ever." I crept around her to direct her view further from Thor. Men can be as devious as women. Men sweetly talk when they think falsely to deceive a female. I needed to regain control. Her children were destined to be the bane of the gods.

It brought me to shame, but I had to serve her with flattery. I preyed on her already damaged character due to Loki's mistreatment. It was successful, but I wished there was another way. Out of her view, I opened a portal to Midgard near Thor. Thor, with all his might, peeled the dreadful snake from the girl. The wolf pup and snake circled my son, but he was ready. The snake sprayed venom towards him but landed on the left side of the pale-faced girl. The sounds of sizzling flesh echoed the room while the girl remained unfazed by that which would cause most agony. Thor ducked and dived toward the snake grasping it by the neck before tossing it through the portal quickly. He knew the death of Angerboda's child would cause her to react, unsure of her power. As this happened, the wolf pup nipped at his calf. He flexed his calf in a rage, which caused the pup's bite to loosen long enough to act. He grabbed the wolf by the scruff and threw it through the portal. He bent down most carefully as he picked up the little girl's still body before taking her through the portal to Midgard.

Angerboda was preoccupied with my captivating words that shrouded Thor's removal of her children. She discovered my deceit which enraged her further. "I'm sorry, Angerboda, but this is necessary. I wish you joy and good health. Those are the best to keep if you can do so without harbouring shame," I informed her, trying to ease the pain I caused.

"My children, my children," she whimpered in reply.

"In Niflheim, you will be reunited with your daughter. It fits with your spider-like look. You will become quite the weaver of more than just webs," I said as I left through the portal to Midgard to join my son with the girl.

As Angerboda cried out in anguish, her form returned to its glory. The beautiful maiden, after nine days and nights of emotional turmoil, stood up in her dark cave. "I am Verdandi!" She screamed like a banshee. The eight realms would know of her power, and even Vanaheim was enlightened to the trick I played. She emerged from the cave and spotted two goblins scurrying through the trees. With a wave of her hands and a rush of wind, their bodies were twisted and reshaped. Skin stretched from their wrists to their hips. Their teeth became elongated and pointed. They wouldn't require a need for food. They shared the thirst for revenge that Verdandi had. She set them to purpose to act her revenge on one of my children. Under the cover of darkness, they moved swiftly through the wilderness.

# A Son's Rise

When we landed in Midgard, I looked around for the children of Loki. To the west, the snake slithered towards the sea, consuming any animal that crossed its path. The serpent grew exponentially, and when it slid beneath the glassy surface, it swam around the world's waters, eating sea creatures of all kinds beneath the waves forever, trying to avoid Thor when he's in pursuit.

Fenrir ran rapidly to the east, towards Jotunheim. He headed towards a familiar figure, a giant with a strong animal resemblance. By the time Fenrir stood toe to toe with another intimidating beast, his size had increased. He bared his teeth at the giant bear with two gigantic claws that roared to show his dominance. This bear was Ullr, and he established a bond with Fenrir sharing an animal spirit. With a face too weary of showing how I felt, I smiled with pride towards my son for standing his ground.

Thor and I made our way to the Bifrost. Suddenly we were surrounded by Draugr without a flame to warn them off, but they acted differently than before. Instead of slashing or trying to devour us, they stood still. Their actions indicated respect, but it wasn't towards me. It was her. They took a knee when they caught a glimpse of the little girl with the half-disfigured face. Thousands of rotting undead soldiers stood eerily silent. Suddenly, each and every single one of them bowed their heads. This gave Thor and I time to safely travel to the entrance of the Bifrost.

I didn't stop as we had to make it back to Asgard. We returned to a concerned look on Ve's face. "Brother, send word to prepare for Njord's arrival. will bring guests," I instructed.

"Odin," he replied quickly. "He is already here, and he brings a gift with his sister and son." I was shocked but relieved all was going well.

"Ok, send for Eir to ensure this girl receives adequate treatment. She will be useful in the dealings with the Draugr," I said, departing towards Valhöll.

On my way to meet Njord, my eldest brother blocked my path. "Vili, I need your sword and your power over the flame," I demanded.

"Is there anything else you need, little king of gods?" Vili mocked.

"Clear the realms of the undead and burn the bodies to ensure the Draugr never rise again," I ordered.

"Ok little Odin. I will do this, but I will gain the throne again, little brother. Or I will burn all that you hold dear," Vili threatened. I turned from him quickly and hastened my pace to welcome Njord to my hall.

As I shoved through the great doors, I was captivated by Jord's beautiful form, though not for long, as I was interrupted by Njord's welcome. He was mocking me in my hall with a sly smirk on his face. "I'm sorry I was not able to welcome you myself, good king," I said respectfully.

"I'm sure you are, wise Odin. I'm sure you are," he stated, handing me the gift. I thanked him gracefully with a bad feeling in my gut. I opened the box, unravelling what was inside. With each layer of cloth, I peeled back a red stain became more prominent. Silence fell in my hall after revealing the box's contents. "Do you think me a fool, Odin? How long did you think the foolish Honir could pretend to be a chieftain?" Njord asked.

My eyes lifted from my uncles severed head to meet Njord's. "To a friend, be a friend, I will repay you one day for this. I only wished to share laughs with you, but your lies and deceit will be met with the same. Why Mimir?" I asked angrily.

"I wished to strike at your heart, Odin. Ve did not do me a dishonour." I slammed my fists on the table out of frustration. "You did not offer an equal gift to gain my family's alliance with Asgard," Njord shouted, raising his voice furiously.

"From now on, I will speak honestly to you, but I'll forever be cautious of your lies. Any more treachery will be repaid with lies," I warned him.

At that moment, I hung my head in shame at failure of my trickery. I was overwhelmed with the sudden flash of visions. The images revealed themselves with the eight claws over the Bifrost. It was Ullr, in bear form, and Fenrir, Loki's son. A range of emotions chased through my mind, with everything unravelling before me. Each step echoed through Asgard. Ullr was a giant of a bear dwarfing myself in comparison, and Fenrir was the size of a horse already. One of the elven guards at my hall attempted to slow their entry, when in an instant, Fenrir bit him in half. Ullr barged through the door and looked down on me in my shame. "Ah, father, Verdandi has told me of your tricks. You have been most unfair. I have come to take the throne from you," Ullr declared.

"How dare you, boy. You will only assume the throne if I decide so. Leave now and take your hideous pet back to Jotunheim," I replied.

"Tomorrow, my two swords against your spear. The victor gains the throne, and the loser will be exiled from Asgard," Ullr stated the terms of the dual boldly. I didn't wish to fight with my son, but regretfully accepted his terms. I had to find a way to win his allegiance, but the throne was my responsibility.

I used the salts and herbs to preserve my uncle's head. My thoughts drifted to my mother. She knew a type of dark magic. She could resurrect Mimir's head to make it useful once more and my mother was the most powerful of all witches that had ascended into the ranks of the Nornir.

Walking through my long hall, I was consumed with thoughts of the dual. I began to doubt if I was right for the throne. There was so much to do.

Ve had left his post to be amongst the people of Midgard under the name of Rig. He created a system of three classes: those that were born great, those that created greatness and those that had greatness thrust upon them. He was an honourable leader in his own right.

Of course, Vili was slaying the dead within the realms; a mighty warrior keen for battle at a moment's notice. He, too, had a desire for the throne. All these questions ran through my head, but I had to stay the course. Warriors can be misled and distracted. Nobility can be mocked in a world of diversity. It was time to focus on the task at hand. I would have to meet my son Ullr on the battlefield.

# The Bear and the Raven

The next day the sun rose, and the battle between father and son cast an eery shadow over Asgard. I walked to my armoury with a heavy head and a heavier heart. The sun glistened on my spear tip, but my gaze was drawn to my shield. I had desired his allegiance and respect. "What will you do, my king?" Jord spoke from behind me.

"When I lose this battle, my lady, you must meet me on an island. This island is where we will have a contest of my knowledge against your love." She smiled at my words. "Take this gift. It will aid you in life by setting you free from the land you get your power from. You will be able to view all you have created from above," I said lovingly, handing over the enchanted cloak of falcon feathers. "One day, I'll ask you for two things, but for now, enjoy your cloak."

After I left the armoury with shield heavy on my arm and my spear gripped tightly, my purpose was clear. I had to fight with honour and lose. I couldn't gain his loyalty through outwitting my son, but I couldn't concede either. There is no honour in walking away from the fight. I had to fight but make it look like Ullr would have true victory.

Entering the arena, I scanned both my surroundings and my opponent. Ullr stood tall wearing his bearskin armour with two swords in his hands. They were like the claws of the animal he resembled. He pounded his chest and roared like a beast, attempting to intimidate its prey before going for the kill.

I now stood in the centre of the arena. My breaths were slow and controlled, with the wind blowing on my face. My feet rooted like an ash tree deep beneath the surface, unknown to all. I scanned around for possible advantages. Each step Ullr took trembled the stadium, but I remained poised, always ready. He circled, keeping my focus on him. When his movements came to an end, he looked into my eyes. He had youth on his side, but experience and adaptability were on mine. I gripped my shield tightly, and my hand on my spear raised, I pointed it at Ullr. "You are big, but I've fought bigger," I said, recalling to the dual with Ymir.

Enraged, my son charged towards me, giving a massive roar on his way, his giant paws were clawing and slashing. I dodged easily, as his fighting pattern was easy to predict. He bombarded me with attacks; however, I began to notice his sword swing slightly weakened every strike he took. Raising my shield, I took a mighty blow from his swords. The impact sent me sliding back a few metres. Now it was time to take charge of the fight and target the areas that were easy to defend. I knew how to beat him, but that was never my aim. A humiliating defeat would never create an ally from foe, so I stabbed my spear toward him, never missing its intent. Suddenly, a stone to the right caught my attention. I attacked and blocked with purpose in mind. Each blow and block manoeuvred my opponent into position until I stood with a rock to my rear.

In an instant, out of frustration and anger, Ullr's swords clashed against my shield once more. This time the blows were slower as if the blades became heavy in his hands. The fight was like a perfect dance with a sword and spear. Each step placed was calculated and quantified accurately. The blow sent me sliding toward the stone, causing me to lose my sure footing. I fell and my son directed his sword toward me while I was at a disadvantage. I could have swept his legs to regain higher ground, but I intended to lose. "That was a good fight, my son. I accept the terms of the fight and will leave. I ask you to accept my shield as a prize for the victory. A King needs to learn sacrifice for the defence of what he holds dear," I said respectfully, accepting my exile.

"Get your things, father, while I allow it," Ullr instructed, drunk with the victory, he caught the eye of the beautiful maiden called Sigyn.

Sigyn was a beautiful shield-maiden, but her love was never true. She was slender with brown hair, olive skin and curves that would leave most men enchanted. She tried her advances on me a few times, but my heart belongs to Jord. Any god or Jotun that attracted this beautiful light elf had her loyalty but only in their victories. As soon as victories waned, her attraction would be lost. This was not a desirable quality in a queen, but that would be my son's lesson to learn. Timing is everything. Whether it is planting seed or giving praise to a child, too much too early will reap an ill harvest.

I addressed the arena of my submission, and the power of control was transferred to Ullr. I was filled with sorrow at the loss of the throne but did not show it. "One day, son, you will learn that the throne requires more sacrifice than freedom. Fairness comes from the heart but doing what is right for the majority comes from the mind," I advised Ullr before retiring to collect my things for the journey ahead.

Jord accompanied me to my room as I gathered my things. Amongst them, I had a magical sack with limitless storage that was a handy tool when wandering the realms. I placed my uncle's head, my spear and a few golden apples from Idunn's orchard. The food I can catch, the water I can find, my wit is all the gear I would need for my inevitable path.

My sight was set on Niflheim, the residence of my mother at her well. The journey was long, and my path had to cross with my brothers as they were needed for Mimir's revival. This would be a family reunion, and much had changed since we all last saw one another at the same time.

The first stop was to pick up Ve, or should I say Rig. My other brother, Vili was slaying undead Jotun within Jotunheim. The mighty sword, Sumarbrandr, danced with foes while he burned those that fell. The path was set and long. Every few days, I rubbed salt to keep my uncles head preserved. I left Asgard with a heavy heart that day, walking over the Bifrost slowly, with my old hall over my shoulder, but much had to be done before I returned. Looking back would have been a waste of time, for I wasn't going that way.

# Family Reunion

Leaving Asgard was always hard, but at least I had one thing to be optimistic about. The island that I informed Jord about is where I would meet my lady. I know her given name was Jord, but now she will always be my lady, my Freya. She taught me lots over the years. She taught me magic with life lessons and failures that would provide the most wisdom. She was beautiful with her red hair and green eyes that were gemstones so precious, I'd call them Gnoss and Gersemi. Her slender figure was deceptive because she had a strength like no other. She was my lady and was always on my mind and in my heart when thinking of the future.

On my way to the island, I visited two homes. One of Agnar and one of Geirrod, to spark the intent for adventure. Each of them to be reunited with their parents once more. Both had a familiar look about them because they went by different names when they were born. Agnar was my double, a spitting image of me at a younger age. Geirrod had a look that somewhat resembled my older brother, Vili. It was time Freya, and I influenced their upbringing. Once I sowed the seeds for travel in them both, their paths intertwined again, and they began their journey to the island.

After our magical reunion, Freya and I waited patiently for our boys. With a strategically placed map and an arranged time, both Agnar and Geirrod met at the boatyard. I made sure they came across a vessel that required two to sail, as a convenient way to ensure both developed a bond while navigating the waters. After their voyage, we welcomed them to our shores and guided them to the feasting table. My lady and I looked at each other, pleased at their upbringing so far. "How about a contest my love?" Freya suggested. There was no honour in backing down from a challenge, so I nodded in agreement.

"I will take Geirrod and teach him the ways of the warrior's mind," I declared, thinking I would win the challenge quickly. Freya smiled like she already knew of her victory.

"And I will take Agnar," she affirmed, knowing it was her most beloved son. "I will teach him the way of the warrior's heart," Freya boasted most confidently.

Agnar spent three days and nights learning from Freya, listening to stories of love, family and home. Those stories were the most valuable gift. It gave lessons of wisdom by inspiring wonder in his mind. The most important reason behind a saga was not only to entertain, but to inspire. Using a tale while inserting wisdom throughout, Agnar learned the reasons why to fight. That which matters most, the love for those you hold dear, the lands where you live and the way of life you wish to keep. Those are the three reasons that inspires conflict from the beginning of time until Ragnarök comes. Love is the very foundation that drives one's warrior spirit and warrior's heart.

My mistake was teaching Geirrod the how and not the why. A warrior must be strong, fit and possess a multitude of skills with weapons and strategies of war. It also took three days to develop his strength, evolve his body and adapt his mind. He climbed mountains, studied hard, and fed to fuel his growth. A warrior in my mind was that with the ability to fight.

After the three days and nights, they boarded their boat setting sail for home. I whispered in the ear of Geirrod. "Be humble enough to be hospitable to those with less. If life gifts you with much, be sure to extend your tables rather than build barriers to those less fortunate." The fool would be ignorant to my advice and not heed my warning and it would be a lesson for me in the end. Freya, and I stayed reserved, as we did not wish to reveal our true identities to our sons. One is destined for glory, riches and a lesson in humility. The other with the thought of love, content and hope. However, destiny has a way of forcing you to become more.

During their voyage home, Geirrod challenged and defeated Agnar in a dual. He tossed him overboard and watched the skinny boy, Agnar, swim back. He was made stronger through his struggle as the waves crashed over him.

Aegir and Ran waited patiently below, but his heart knew there were better things ahead. Each stroke took him closer to home. He swam for three days, and by the time he made it to the shore, Geirrod had already become General of the army. Agnar lived in peace unaffected by the rise of the close friend who betrayed him. He simply wished for a simple life, but his mother and I had other plans.

Three years later, their paths crossed again. Geirrod was now a king, and he did not recognise the brother that sailed with so long ago. Drunk with victory and spoiled by wealth and position, King Geirrod reduced Agnar to a mere stable boy. He would have to tend to his horses while Geirrod celebrated his riches and fame.

Geirrod was a great warrior, but his elevated position and his ego made him numb to my words. He became bitter and greedy of power and wealth until one day I came calling. I dressed as an old man with a walking staff and blue cloak, then entered the king's stables and came across Agnar, my son. Most wouldn't recognise the young man that had come to the island years ago, but I did, as my all-seeing eyes could see more than most.

"Ah, Agnar, why do you sweep stables for the king? Your mother wanted more for you," I spoke curiously about his purpose.

"Do I know you, weary wanderer?" He replied, trying to figure out my true identity.

"I know of you, boy, and I don't think you were meant for such mediocre tasks," I said.

"Oh really, old man, and what is your purpose here? Other than mocking me," Agnar replied with quick wit.

"A meal with the king, boy. A meal with the king. I gifted to him years ago, and the least he can do is share a meal with an old man," I said cryptically.

"Do not go to him. His wealth and position have twisted him into a cruel ruler," Agnar warned.

"The unworthy abuse their power. Once the bold rise up, the power they abuse will be removed from them," I said, as I did not fear what was going to happen when I left the stables.

I hobbled towards the feasting room. Through the secret passage behind the fireplace. "What do you want, old man?" Geirrod asked impolitely.

"Just a meal for this weary wanderer, king," I replied as I kept up the appearance of my disguise.

"Guards!! Get him out of my hall," he demanded. He was too blinded by his successes to recall the warnings I gave to him long ago.

"You will regret this. You are unworthy of kingship in comparison to another. Even a mere stable boy would do a better job than you," I cursed as I was assisted out of the castle. My words were always carefully picked and structured. I knew I had said enough to cause a reaction to confirm Freya, the victor of our little challenge.

The king, angry at my curse, marched to the stables to confront Agnar. To Geirrod's surprise, Agnar stood his ground. He never had much skill but fought back regardless. The battle was epic. Geirrod had more skill and fighting ability, but Agnar had a fire inside like no other. A true warrior's spirit: a light within that kept him fighting. With each blow he received, he stood up to fight again and again and again. Geirrod was smug with his ability. He dropped his guard for only an instant, but it was enough to change the fight's outcome. Agnar stood victorious over Geirrod while his warriors watched the defeat.

I was in the back whispering words to Geirrod's commanders to change their loyalty towards Agnar. When the defeated king asked for help from his men, they provided help, but not as he wished from them. Instead, he was helped to his feet and exiled from the kingdom. The warriors and generals cheered for Agnar as he stood battered and broken. I riled everyone to celebrate the victory, chanting Agnar's name. "Agnar is no kings name, stable warrior," said one of the men.

"Your victory earned your title. You shall be known as king Sigurd," another warrior said.

"Hail king Sigurd!!" They exclaimed loudly over and over again. Freya had triumphed over me, and our son Baldur became a king of men. Geirrod would be back for another attempt to reclaim his throne. Blinded by jealousy, Hödr would face his brother again.

# Three Brothers Return Home

I departed king Sigurd to seek out my brother, Rig, journeying until one morning, I saw his character leave the residence of a couple. "Brother! I need you now," I declared, setting him to pause from his hasty retreat.

"Lost the throne, brother, and you need my help to reclaim it?" He asked with a smug look on his face.

"No, I need you to help with this," I said while pulling our uncle's head from my bag.

"We need to find Vili if we are going to attempt this kind of magic again," Rig informed me of what I already knew.

"Let us head to Jotunheim then," I said while rubbing more salt and herbs on the severed head.

The journey to Jotunheim was lengthy and challenging like it always was, but the flames of Vili blazed like a trail of breadcrumbs. The ashes and embers of the burned Draugr led us to our warrior brother. Ve and I broke through the dense pine trees to access a clearing. We followed the sounds of blades clashing and fire blazing filled the air in Jotunheim. "Vili! We need you now, brother," I shouted as my eyes gained sight of him.

"Ah, little brother, so far from the throne. Word spreads quicker than fire about your defeat. You have no authority over me or anyone anymore," Vili said smugly. As I pulled Mimir's head from my bag, the fire in his eyes blazed, and his temper followed. "Who did this?" He demanded to know.

"It doesn't matter. What matters is how we fix it," Ve said, trying to soothe Vili's ignorant rage.

"You mean her? She will not be pleased to see us brothers. She hasn't been happy since we slew Ymir," Vili cautioned us to the dangers of our mission.

"She is our mother. Surely our intentions for her brother might mend things from the past," I said reassuringly.

"She goes by Urd now, and she is much more than the mother we once knew," Ve said.

My brothers and I left the enormous mountains of Jotunheim behind with its dark forests and rocky terrain. Niflheim was the destination in mind, that cold and dark landscape where it all began and where snow and ice were as far as Ve's eyes could see.

We crossed the land for three days and nights through the blizzards caused us to move aimlessly through the snow. Until our last step, when most would have lost hope, the ice cracked beneath us. "Don't move!" I said, causing my brothers to freeze on the spot. Still, the crack echoed beneath our feet. Suddenly, it gave way beneath, sending all of us sliding into long, open tunnels beneath the ice. We twisted and turned, becoming separated from each other, but eventually landed together in a cave. There we saw a unique ash tree standing unaffected by the harsh climate. This tree had a portal-like door, but we only viewed it from afar. We scanned our surroundings for possible threats before deciding to proceed further. I always checked my flanks in unknown territory.

"Boys," an eery voice echoed around the cave. "You dare return here after all that you have done?" It asked. Suddenly a withered lady Jotun appeared from behind the tree.

"Mother, we have not come to fight about the past. We have come for help towards the future," I said as I revealed her brother's head.

"What you ask is the darkest of magic. It'll come at a great cost to all of you and you will be changed forever. This decision will rip you three apart and lead to Ragnarök." The last word sent a cold shiver up our spines.

"What is Ragnarök? I asked curiously.

"Ragnarök is the inevitable end for all things. It is unavoidable and inescapable. Before the great battle between the realms begins, you will ask your uncle's head one last question. It has happened before and will happen again," Urd said.

"What will come to pass?" I asked.

"A giant wolf will devour the sun and moon. There will be nothing but cold and darkness for the lands and this time will last for three ages. It will be known as Fimbulwinter. Brother will kill brother, fathers will kill children, and children will kill fathers. Chaos will battle the forces of control, and the worlds will burn and sink into Ymir's blood again."

"What hope do we have in such times?" I asked, clutching at a thread of hope to hold.

"Some will survive just like the death of Ymir. Your sons and your sons' sons will rise to rule, but only if you influence it in such a way that life will prosper. You have a great choice to make, Odin: the choice of who will succeed you on the throne."

Thoughts ran through my mind as I handed over the head of Mimir. Urd snatched it from my hands and proceeded to carry it toward the ash tree. She dipped the head in the water at her well beneath the tree's base. She would wet the roots regularly, using the waters of her well. She spoke the magical enchantments repeatedly, and the well began to glow. "Now, quickly go through this portal to Jotunheim. It will take you to Mimir's home, where an enemy lies in wait. Send her to me as she is my sister in this world. Verdandi has a score to settle with you, Odin," Urd warned.

We all stepped through the doorway in the tree, and we appeared through the door of another tree. It was Mimir's place, the garden outside his home. It was nighttime, damp and gloomy. Whispers were faint, and the fog was thick. Something was moving in the shadows. It was moving quickly like a moment in the present, come and gone instantly.

Unexpectedly, Verdandi rushed us, but we overpowered her. It was unfortunate for her that when my brothers and I stood together, nothing would stand a chance. Collectively we restrained her just long enough to send her through the doorway that remained open. It closed behind Verdandi and that is where she would stay. Returning my focus to my uncle's head, I called my brothers to perform the magic used to create Askr and Embla. Vili gave the head intelligence, Ve gave it the ability to see, hear and speak, and I gave Mimir's head life once more. He began to regain consciousness and regurgitated the water he was submerged in from Urd's well so much so, that he created a large pool of water at the base of the ash tree.

# Gift for a Gift

Mimir's well was filling from the waters of wisdom as he brought back knowledge from beyond death. All three of us stood back in awe, as the waters neared the brim, Mimir began to cough and splutter the remaining liquid from Urd's well. "Nephews, you brought me back, but how?"

"Your sister, our mother helped. How do you feel? What lessons from beyond do you have for us?" I asked while trying to figure out if it was the same uncle I knew from before.

"A gift for a gift, smart nephew, a gift for a gift," Mimir said as his smile widened.

"Name the price. I will gladly pay," I said, perhaps a little too eager with my thirst for knowledge.

"Well, young one, go get my Gjallarhorn. The horn from the great Ymir, fill it with the liquid in the well and drink it. Drink it all, and you will gain power unlike any other. The knowledge of everyone's death before your own. But this power comes with caution Odin. Let no man know his fate. It will rob him of the joys of experience in the present. The cost, one of your all-seeing eyes," Mimir said without a smile or any hints of humour. The very terms sent a chill down my spine, but courage was acting despite the fears presented to us.

Grabbing my knife from my belt, I hacked out my payment, letting out a scream, I dropped to my knees. The pain was unimaginable, and my brothers stood back in awe. Crawling towards the well, I clutched the Gjallarhorn while I dangled my eye above. As it dropped into the waters, I filled the horn and drank it dry. As if by the intoxication of the well, the power rushed into the gaping, eye socket. Winds lifted me off my feet. My missing eye illuminated the entire cave. The rush of power was like a lightning storm amid a hurricane, but passed in an instant, making it feel like a millennia before I stood again on solid ground.

"Step forward, Ve," Mimir instructed. "And what power do you seek?"
"Uncle, I have created the different classes of mortals, and my senses are so sharp I can hear the grass grow on Midgard from Asgard," Ve said proudly.

"After hearing the prophecy of Ragnarök, the only power I'd like is allowing all to know Ragnarök has begun."

"A gift for a gift, young Ve, a gift for a gift," Mimir said. "My well has an all-seeing eye to keep it updated with visual input, but it can't hear. Your great hearing ability will keep it full and useful in the time to come. Take the horn that Odin used, and the power will be yours. You will be heard in the nine realms when Ragnarök is upon us." Ve grabbed my knife and sliced his ear off. With a shrieking scream of agony, while his hacked off appendage was placed in the well. It sank in the watery depths. He grabbed the horn and raised it high in triumph. With a rush of light and magic that illuminated the entire cave once more, Ve looked entirely different. He was pale and very serious. His teeth became golden, and if he spoke, it would always be valuable to listen to him.

Vili stepped forward, "half blind and half deaf, and they can see more and hear more than before," Vili laughed condescendingly. "I am the greatest and eldest of the sons of Bor. I have defeated the Draugr single-handedly. I deserve the power of control and to become the rightful ruler of the eight realms, not nine. I and I alone deserve the power to burn those that stand against my rule," Vili demanded.

"Ah, eldest son of Bor, if it is power you seek, you shall have to roam to gain it. First, I require a gift for a gift, Vili," Mimir said with a lifeless expression.

"My sword that can fight on its own. That'll be a worthy gift for the power to destroy my foes," Vili spoke, thinking that power would be his and the need for weaponry would no longer be required.

"Take this ring on your journey, Vili. It is a weapon that will make you a king: a perfect circle, no end and no beginning; a continuous cycle is like time itself. But heed this warning Vili, everything must die. Everything must end so something else can take its place to make it better. Your time will end like everyone else, but the power you seek lies in Muspelheim. Something there started all of this, and the only way you can ensure your longevity is by having this power on your side. But be cautious eldest son of Bor. The ring, like time, holds alliance to no one. Go now. You will find access to Muspelheim in the lands of sand," Mimir's voice filled his soul with purpose.

Vili left immediately to travel the eight realms in his quest for unbeatable power. My brother and I took our gifts and left for the shores of

Jotunheim. We had to return to Asgard once more as someone was in my seat. It wouldn't be easy to regain my throne, so I had some thinking to do.

When we got to the coast, we sat on the beach watching the wave maidens role in and out. We joked around with nicknames for each other by appearances. "King wink," Ve said while laughing.

"Sorry, Ear," I replied with a smile on my face.

"There's a Valkyrie that goes by that name," Ve said, returning us to serious discussions about titles. "Can you tell me my fate, brother?" he asked, and as I cast my gaze upon him, a flood of images of swords clashing and armour gleaming there was the revelation of who would cause his death. A familiar but sinister smile appeared from behind his foe's blade.

"I can't," I said to Ve while seeing the truth. "If I did, you'd seek to challenge it or avoid It, causing it to come to pass regardless." Ve had a look of amazement on his face as if he had seen something quite spectacular.

"I have your name, brother. Odin, the one with the flaming eye. Your eye socket just then burned brighter than the fires of Muspelheim." I liked it because it paid homage to my new power.

"And I have a name for you, brother. It came to me in my vision," I said as the wave maidens climbed onto the shore only to be pulled back into the depths. "Heimdall, the watcher. You will be the security for the homes of all. You will stand at the edge of the Bifrost, looking for threats within the realms. You will be the guardian of the world, the noblest of all brothers. Fitting your gold teeth because if you speak, your words are of much worth, brother."

On our long journey over the oceans and through Midgard, I had finally concocted a plan. It would not only gain me my throne but leave me with my son's allegiance. His weakness was his companion Fenrir. His loyalty to his friend was most dreadful for everyone in the eight realms. And that was a weakness that could be exploited.

# The Return of the Yulefather

We eventually made it to our destination in Midgard. Far from the eyes of mortals, Heimdall called forth the Bifrost. I was glad to be heading home after such a long exile, as much had been accomplished. At that moment, I gazed at my reflection in the water, the socket where my eye once began to illuminate, and I saw my fate. It ended in the jaws of a massive wolf, which made my thoughts drift to the wolf pup I crossed paths with so long ago. "How could it be so big? The unnatural beast did grow quick, but it should have plateaued," I thought to myself.

I left my brother at his home, Himinbjörg, at the edge of the Bifrost, but my vision caused concern. "Hello, Odin," said an unfamiliar voice from the shadows. As I turned to find the origin of the greeting, my eye spotted her in the darkness.

"Hel!! How are you, little girl?" I asked while seeing the sweet little girl I saved so long ago.

"Not good, Odin. The other gods are uncomfortable around me, but when the Draugr see me, they treat me like a queen," she mumbled with a hopeless look on her half-decayed face. I recalled her unique power over the Draugr so long ago and how they seemed to respect her presence.

"Perhaps I have a role for you yet, but first, I need to reclaim the throne," I said, consoling her in her unhappiness. I left to initiate my plan, but when I got closer to my old hall, the sound of a wolf howl echoed around Asgard. I was unsure of what awaited, but I had to proceed regardless of the dangers ahead.

Marching up to the doors of Valhöll, I barged through with purpose. As soon as I laid my eye on my son, I caught a glimpse of his fate. The image of it rushed into my head like a sudden headache. It was a strange vision. He only had one hand, and he'd face a shared fate with me. The jaws of a giant wolf would claim his life, which brought me both joy and sadness. I knew he'd be on my side in the end, but no father should see his son die. It looked like my gift was also the curse of foresight.

"Ah, father, welcome back. Have you come to claim your throne back?" Ullr asked, sitting in the chair smugly.

"Not yet, boy," I said, bowing my head in respect. Suddenly, the howling in the distance started, followed by earth-shaking footsteps. There were four steps in succession, then a break for a while.

"He's hungry again," Ullr said, frustrated. "We only fed him three moons ago, and he took two of my guards." I was beginning to wonder who was ruling who.

We departed Valhöll tall wooden structure built from the shields of fallen warriors to look toward the source of the howl. Suddenly, there he was: a wolf the size of a mountain, casting shadows and darkness overall. Fenrir was an intimidating sight and could not be destroyed as Ymir once was. With my new abilities, perhaps tempting fate would be foolish. It's wyrd because the attempt of killing Fenrir would taunt the fate sisters. Taking direct action on Fenrir would forfeit Ullr's life before the big bad wolf would come for mine.

"Not much of a king you are, boy. Forever a slave to that devourer of a beast," I said sternly.

"He's my friend father," Ullr replied.

"Be a friend to my friends and me. Don't be a friend to my enemies," I said wisely. "You rule because of him, and others live in fear. He doesn't destroy everything because you are constantly feeding him. It would be best if you could control your pet, boy," I warned him of that which he already came to realise. Ullr turned to his men and sent them to fetch the fetters that would bind Fenrir.

"I will play on the ego of the mighty wolf, father," Ullr said as we headed to face and feed the mighty Fenrir. The walk was long. As we entered his shadow, his breath surrounded us with the stench of death. The great feast was presented to the beast. There were nine whales piled high in front of the monstrous wolf.

"Mighty wolf hungry again, I see," Ullr said.

"Mighty bear king apologies. My size requires much sustenance," Fenrir replied, and then his gaze turned to me. "What is he doing here?" Fenrir snarled as he began to bare his teeth.

"He has returned and is my guest," Ullr said, drawing his attention from my presence. "Before we feed you this time, I present a challenge to you, my mighty friend," Ullr suggested as one of the elves came with the chains.

"Oh, I like games. My strength will be legendary, even more than Thor's," the wolf boasted. The chains were thrown over the beast and secured tightly. Fenrir shook his massive body one, and the chain was reduced to shards, causing metal to fly around the world.

"That was pathetic," Thor said, unimpressed by the might of the wolf. Fenrir tossed the remainder of the chains off quickly before he devoured nine whales and left with no words of thanks.

Unknown to all, except myself, a single hair fell from the mighty beast when he made a mockery of the chain. Once it floated down to the ground, I gathered it up and kept it in my pocket.

When the wolf was out of sight, and the footsteps could no longer be felt, Ullr returned to the forge of Asgard. "Make the chain again, but this time, I want it to be three times stronger," Ullr instructed the sons of Ivaldi. The elves of Alfheim were my creations, and Ivaldi was an elven term for Allfather. They began to work on the second, thicker chain and made sure to make it heavier than their previous creation.

"Another attempt to trap the mighty Fenrir will be made," Ullr declared as the elves and gods cheered in hope with the more fortified chain's completion.

It was only three more moons that passed before the howling returned, ringing like a dinner bell around Asgard. "Dinner time again? What will you feed him when the whales run out?" I asked Ullr. His face showed signs of concern as if he had never thought of the inevitable. "What will it take? The elves? The humans? The animals? If this continues, life, as we know it, will cease to exist." The gods began to side with me as my words rang true in their hearts.

"This chain will work," Ullr said confidently.

We left to meet the wolf once more on the edge of Asgard. The gods gathered as Ullr presented the second challenge to his mighty friend. "Would this earn your respect, Thor?" Fenrir asked.

"It is a mighty chain. I am the only one who can lift it, but even I can't break this one," Thor informed the great wolf. Fenrir seemed bigger than before as if with everything he devoured, he gained more size to accommodate. Thor began to fasten the chains to the mighty wolf, being sure to secure them as tightly as he was able.

The challenge began as the gods and elves looked on with smiles in the hope of success. I remained reserved, as the wolf's size and strength had increased substantially since our last attempt. It was as if each meal empowered the wolf, causing growth and development. Fenrir stretched and pushed, but the bonds held. This made everyone's smiles grow wider. As Fenrir spotted his friend taking joy in his struggle, his rage grew. He twisted and turned furiously while the bonds creaked and groaned in their attempts to hold him. With one mighty display of strength, the chains broke. The joy he saw in his struggles created a hatred like no other and this hate was directed to Asgard and his old friend Ullr. This challenge caused Fenrir to shed another hair that I gathered quickly.

"The next attempt to prove my strength will cost you a gesture of goodwill, old friend," Fenrir scowled at the bear king before his earth-shaking footsteps bounded away into the distance.

Later that day, the gods gathered in council and feast. "A king that can't control his pet," Njord mocked.

"At leassst when Odin was in power, he had thingsss more in control than you," Loki spoke from the back of the room.

"Gods, you should not mock another. Respected are those that do not focus on others' failures," I said to silence the pettiness. They were right, though, I had more control over the realms than Ullr did. Ullr roared before slamming his fist on the table.

"I am fair. If any have suggestions, I am open to listening," Ullr stated.

"Ease yourself, son, when you reach your boiling point. Fenrir will grin, and your council won't be delivered with a snapped bowstring. Don't be pigheaded, as your knowledge will be disregarded like cawing crows. Your peace of mind is lost and can be visually seen by others," I said to king Ullr.

"Make the chainsssss bigger," Loki hissed.

"Perhaps the mighty Loki can attach the bigger chains next time," Thor said sarcastically. Loki shrank back and came to silence, dwindling back to the edge of the room.

"Perhaps wise Odin knows what to do," Njord said, looking to test me.

"I do, but each of you gods should know that only fools think that all who laugh are a friend. When the time comes to call for support, few will come to your aid. If I do this and return with a solution, I want what is rightfully mine," I said, staring at Ullr with my one good eye. The room fell into silence as everyone turned to look at him. His face was blank, but he decided it was the right thing to do.

"Very well. What do you need from us?" He asked.

"Loki and I shall seek out the king of dwarves in Svartalfheim. We shall return before the third full moon with what we need," I said, rising from my chair with purpose.

# Need is Better than Desire

When I was in Ullr's company, Vili was out on his mission for power. He had nothing but the clothes on his back, his wits and the magic ring he gained. The journey was so long, that with every step he took, his feet ached and caused him great pain. His souls were covered in blood from burst blisters and were torn to shreds from the rocky paths taken over high mountains and through dark woods. The pain wasn't enough to slow his pace or alter his thinking, though. His desire for power was the wind in his sails and it was all that he required to continue on a path filled with pain and lesson.

When he finally reached the barren wasteland of Muspelheim, his unique ability allowed him to continue unburned. The flame of the sun simmered his flesh from above as the sand baked him from below. Muspelheim was the most dangerous place compared to every other terrain in the eight realms because of the intense heat. He stumbled wearily in his pain until he reached the grand opening in a volcano now called Emi Koussi. He staggered exhausted through a dark door as every step he mustered echoed in the large cavern.

"What brings you to my domain, son of Bor?" The voice asked as it trembled the volcanic cave.

"I seek a power! A power that will make me a king!" Vili yelled in reply. A low rumble shook the foundation of the massive volcano as a wingless dragon rose from the lava. It looked him in the eyes, grinning.

"I am Nidhoggr, and I started everything when I was only a child. I am the most powerful being in creation, for I am time personified. No matter your successes or failures in life, with one swift swoop, all will be gone," the dragon's voice boomed through the entire realm.

"You are powerful, Nidhoggr, but you are trapped in this cave. What if I gave you the ability to fly? Would you make me a king?" The dragon paused to ponder the offer for a moment. An eerie, malevolent silence filled the air. The only noise that could be heard was the scales of the dragon screening and groaning as it moved.

"Give me what you offer, and I'll make you a king," Nidhoggr said cryptically.

Vili waved his hands and chanted magical incantations that granted flight to the mighty dragon. The dragon dropped to its knees in agony as lumps rippled across his back while he groaned and struggled through the discomfort. With one mighty roar as he stretched up, his wings burst through from his back. "Hmmm, interesting," he said whilst admiring his new tools for freedom.

"And now my power. Hold up your end of the bargain, beast!" Vili demanded loudly.

"Easy son of Bor. I will grant what you wish. You will become king of this place. Because one must remain until Ragnarök comes."

Nidhoggr pulled his head back as he inhaled the deepest of breaths. A bright glow came from the back of his mouth just before he sprayed Vili with flames. The fire scorched his very skin, but with this new power, he began to grow in size and strength. The longer he spent in the breath of Nidhoggr, the larger he became. Vili's skin was charred, and while surrounded by fire, his thoughts drifted back to his uncle's words. He reached into his pocket and pulled out the ring. His eyes were drawn to its simplicity and beauty. The golden ring had a rune glowing bright red amongst the flame. It was Naudiz.

Now knowing Nidhoggr had deceived him, he raised the ring high in the air and roared so loud. It stopped the dragon's breath for a moment and with a flash of light, Nidhoggr was absorbed into the ring, and it received its curse.

Vili looked at the ring and realised the power he got wasn't exactly what he wanted. He became the king of Muspelheim but was unable to leave until the sun has been devoured. He was a ruler but not of the kingdom he wished. He suspected that I would reclaim the throne once more, which infuriated him further. It appeared that Mimir's gift of wisdom to Vili was a great riddle, indeed. The power of time is on no one's side. The devotion to time will leave you burned out in life, as power is attained through action, honour and mutual respect. Power is not for those who rule over others, but a power to gift your kin with wisdom and learning through the chaos of life.

Vili ignorantly threw the ring as hard as possible, sending it across the skies and through the stars. The cursed ring flew through the realms like a comet only to end in a pile of treasure. This pile of riches belonged to a mighty and cunning dwarf, Andalfari. Beneath the moving curtains of a waterfall, the ring will remain hidden to the world.

Andalfari guarded the treasure against everyone who dared to come close and earned his wealth through his triumphs of bravery against kings of dwarves, Jotuns and elves. He was sly but thriving in all his adventures, but my fate drew me toward the ring, and our paths would cross again one day.

Vili was left alone to wander in the hottest of all the realms. The barren desert wasteland, that if any unfortunate person were to become lost in this realm, their bodies would become ash. During his wandering, he came across a giant piece of metal and took it back to his volcanic cave. He began beating the metal hard with his massive fists. His hard strikes pounded the metal, causing it to fold and bend to his will. Farbauti, the hard striker, was his name, and within the realm of heat, he would manufacture his great sword. The blade would be used to hold those sent to him while they burned and became sons of Muspelheim. He would continue to sharpen and hone his weapon until he marched toward Asgard at Ragnarök when the time approached.

Meanwhile, in Asgard, something quite sinister lurked in the shadows. She crept in the darkness, silently and quickly like a shadow. She was far more powerful than I and moved with purpose. During her exile in Niflheim, she had learned magic spells from my mother, Urd, that increased her power and threat tenfold. This witch took two things I saved for a later time that would be my downfall. The hairs of the Fenrir would be used to herald in Ragnarök, something I was trying desperately to delay.

I looked powerless to act as Verdandi returned to her ironwoods to begin her spell casting. Time was at least on my side until the wolves were ready to start their pursuit.

# Travelling Far and Wide

The path was long and hard, as most are on the journey to wisdom. The wisdom learned in life is obtained through overcoming complicated pathways through long journeys and challenging climbs. An easy journey does not leave lasting lessons, and being young and travelling in solitude might lead you down the wrong trails, to whereas travelling with others can bring aid and different teachings of wisdom.

Loki and I crossed over the Bifrost into Midgard, stopping at the edge of Svartalfheim. The mountainous terrains with forests and cave systems contain dwarves and goblins. During our journey through Midgard, we made a fire at the river's edge to keep the Draugr away. "What a beautiful animal in the water there," Loki said to spark some conversation. My all-seeing eye noticed that there was magic surrounding that swimming animal.

"Yes, it is a beautiful creature, Loki, and so it should remain. Never try and obtain instant perfection. Instead, it is wise to get something and make it better. Reliance and pride should come from your efforts alone, not another's," I said, knowing it fell on deaf ears. Loki was mesmerised by the Otter's brown fur shimmering in the light.

Loki separated back to the two wolves he once was. Their mouths drooled as they began to stalk their prey.

You should never steal another's love. It happens way too often.

The Otter's beauty was more than skin deep, but foolish Loki remained ensnared by the vision of the pelt. I managed to stop one by using my food supplies to feed it, but Geri was too greedy and dived into the shallow part of the river to kill the otter. As jaws clamped down on the poor animal, and my thoughts were drawn to my shared fate. Once Geri returned to the bank, I became concerned about my lack of control of that side of Loki. Freki was more obedient and respectful. Her hunger could be satisfied.

Freki began to move closer to her brother, as if Geri was hailing her to. As she stepped closer to the wolf standing over the otter's remains, their bodies twisted and merged. The sounds of bones breaking and wolves struggling filled the campsite. Suddenly, Loki was standing in front of me once more. "What have you done, Loki?" I asked, disappointed with his inability to follow instructions.

"I wanted it sssooo I took it," he hissed as he grabbed his knife from his belt. He began to remove the beautiful skin from the animal and use it as a scarf. The meat was cooked for a meal that night, but I gave mine to Loki, as I couldn't stomach the devouring of a dwarf in otter form.

"That'll catch up to you, Loki," I cautioned as he continued to tear at the meat that was cooked rare.

When morning came, we continued to the king of the dwarves. King Hreidmar was a good king, but his lust for gold and wealth was his curse.

Better gear and good sense a traveller can carry. Better than riches are for the wretched.

As we eventually made it to the ruler's doors, we asked the guard to announce our arrival to the king. After a short while, we were escorted up to the throne room. The king's sons were by his side, but all had a stern look of grief and anger fall across their faces. Their eyes focused on Loki's new scarf. "You come here to ask for something while your companion wears my son's skin around his neck. You must think me a fool to ever align myself with you treacherous gods," Hreidmar roared at us.

"Forgive me, great king. Kids are a great gift of life even to parents without much to give. He is now an ancestor, hopefully inspiring his brothers to build their own road in life. I humbly ask how I can remedy this situation?" I asked, bowing and pulling Loki into a bow also. My eye could see that Fafnir gripped his axe tightly, preparing to take vengeance. Regin drew his dagger from its pouch and, with his thin stick-like arm, pointed at us eagerly.

Hreidmar rose from his throne and proceeded to say, "if you can give me a treasure that can account for every hair on the pelt, I will forgive the loss of my son." My all-seeing eye had caught a glimpse of such horde on our journey.

"It is better to be responsible for your path in life rather than to rely on others while your life dwindles at the fireplace, good king. I'll send Loki to retrieve the treasure for the compensation you require. I shall remain here as a token of good faith that he returns with debt paid." The sons looked shocked at my response, but not even a king can rescind an offer when it's already been declared. I leant over to whisper the location of Andalfari's treasure to Loki. "Start where your actions lead to this path. Follow the river's rapid race, and when it appears to end, you'll be at your destination," I whispered cryptically enough for the sons not to attempt to beat Loki to the treasure. "Take this magical bag, Loki. It can hold more than it looks."

Loki left the throne room, and when he had gotten beyond the kingdom walls, he morphed into Geri and Freki once more. Their pace hastened quickly across the countryside, over hills and through forests until he returned to where he killed Otter Hreidmarson. Once there, the wolves transformed back into Loki. He began to ponder my cryptic words, thinking back to my instructions and followed the direction of the river. It went for miles down through forest and field.

Just as the landscape appeared to come to an end, Loki recalled my instructions once more. "I'm here," he thought to himself. He peered over to reveal the water began to fall to a lower level. "Ah, waterfall, simple name but does the trick. Things don't have to be over complicated when it comes to names. Now to climb down the....," he paused to think of another name. "Bank, yesss the riverbank. Well, I am collecting gold," he said to himself, thinking himself funny and intelligent. Once he returned to his task, he recalled my instructions a third time, looking at the waterfall and admired shimmering in the water. Loki grasped at the sparkling water, thinking it was the gold I was after. He soon realised a cave beyond, but also noticed a pike in the water below stalked him closely.

Loki entered carefully, avoiding a fall into the pike's territory. He uncovered the treasure required to cover every hair on his otter's pelt., grabbing and clutching at the riches, quickly throwing them into the magical sack I gave him. Loki gathered every piece of gold and jewel hastily until he caught a glimpse of it: a treasure unlike any other. It was a ring that was unique in power and beauty. However, it was the power that attracted Loki more than its beauty. He was mesmerised and time stood still, causing him to shake his head to regain his senses. Loki became unhealthily attached to the item. His desire was great, he lusted after it and he kept the ring on his person. Power tends to corrupt those who are not wise enough to use it.

Loki left the cave and emerged from behind the waterfall, stopping to admire his new ring on the riverbank. In the water, something stirred, and in an instant, something from the murky depths of the stream breached the surface. The pike transformed mid-air into Andalfari the dwarven warrior with a sword in hand. "Give me the treasure you took," he demanded. Loki smiled disrespectfully and morphed into Geri and Freki once more.

The two wolves circled the mighty dwarf. Salivating and growling at their prey, they waited for the perfect moment to strike. Andalfari stood his ground, keeping them at bay. Each attempt Geri or Freki lunged towards him, was blocked with shield and sword. In a swift moment, Andalfari gained the upper hand. He knocked the wolves to the ground, and they became Loki again.

"Here, take the sack," Loki said while his eyes grinned. Andalfari bent down to collect the sack, but instead, he received eyes full of gravel. As the dwarven warrior stumbled, Loki threw the otter skin at the dwarf casting a curse. As he dropped to his knees in pain, Andalfari's body twisted and reshaped into a horse.

This horse was unique. His blade in his hand became a horn on his head. The beauty galloped away from Loki as quickly as it could.

When Loki retrieved the pelt and put the ring on, he could see his father burning in Muspelheim. The ring gave him power and the ability of fire was absorbed by one of the wolves inside.

He left and headed back to pay the death debt required for Gleipnir's construction.

# A Gift to Make Amends

Returning to the edge of the King Hreidmar's boundary, Geri and Freki morphed into Loki. He was escorted up to the king's hall and presented the magical sack to the king. "Ah yes, the bag contains enough gold for each hair on my son's skin. It looks like Loki was successful in his ventures," Hreidmar said while his eyes were enslaved to Loki's new ring. Once the brothers had the magical sack, they began counting the pieces of gold and silver until the impossible price was paid. "Ah, so the debt has been pain, Odin. Now, what do you wish we construct for you?" The king asked.

"We require a strong bond to restrain the mighty Fenrir. Two chains failed before. The latter of great strength and thickness, but he still broke free," I informed the king.

"Silly gods, we have harvested the finest of materials, and can create such a bond that even the largest of beasts cannot break. Verdandi's web was used to manufacture a silk ribbon. It is delicate but stronger than any material in the realms. Every stretch or attempt to escape causes its strength to increase, but it will require some Ingredients from the gods to enchant it further," the king said with a smile.

"That sounds exceptional, please give me the ingredients, and I'll make sure it is done," I replied in haste.

"Not so fast, Lord Odin. First, we will require payment for such a thing," Hreidmar said as his eyes lit up at Loki's new ring. He was always fixated on gold and things of value.

"Greedy king, it is unwise not to know your limits when it comes to wealth. Saving to excess can turn a friend into a foe. Will Loki's ring be sufficient payment?" I asked, looking towards Loki's hand. The ring bore familiarity to me, resembling Mimir's ring given to my brother years ago. I was right to believe fate desired for us to cross paths once more.

"Loki, give the king your ring," I instructed.

"Bu…but… it'ssss mine," Loki said.

"Better gear and good sense a traveller can carry. Riches are for the wretched," I instructed as I clutched Loki's wrist and removed it from his finger, relieving him from the effects of the trinket. When I touched it, I received a vision. It was an image of the power inside this ring. Tooth, claw and fire, the vision of a mighty dragon inside made me hesitant on handing it over, as I knew Fenrir was the more immediate problem than the ring's curse. I handed it over to the king and I saw the devious looks Fafnir and Regin were giving. Their gaze followed the ring to their father's hand. Hreidmar handed over the silken ribbon with an obscure list of ingredients. I scanned it, deciphering such cryptic components for the enchantments needed. Leaving with Loki, I warned the king. "That ring is cursed, and it will bring you great misfortune. Heed my words, King. Get rid of it before bad things happen."

Loki and I left quickly. It had been two new moons since we had left Asgard, and by the third, Fenrir would return.

It wasn't long before the sons of Hreidmar killed their father. Such sad tidings when families quarrel over money or power.

Fafnir was the mightiest of the two sons to claim the sack full of treasure. The battle was one-sided, but Regin won Fafnir's blade as a result of his efforts. Unfortunately, Mimir's damned ring gave his brother a far superior power than anything Regin could muster. They knew the ring was a cursed, but still did not let that sway their coveting of it.

As we left that wretched place, I knew that I would have to return the ring to my uncle at a later time, as its power twisted and mutated Fafnir's physical form. Regin escaped Fafnir's new appearance into Midgard. There he would plan and plot to one day lay his crafty hands on the ring again.

# The Cost of the Silk Ribbon

It was the day before the third new moon that Loki and I returned. We hastened our movements and sent word for a gathering of gods to decrypt the ingredients needed for Gleipnir. The sound of a cat's footsteps, the breath of a fish, roots of a mountain, spittle of a bird, the beard of a woman and the sinews of a bear. My mind raced to look for answers to such things.

"Ssssounds like animal sssacrifice to me," Loki suggested.

"Not that easy, boy. Hreidmar is more cunning than that," I replied.

The gods began to convene in Valhöll. Freya was first to cross the threshold, causing my mind to recall the first ingredient on the list. Freya always travelled with her two cats drawing her chariot. "My lady, I need your magic to trap Fenrir. The first ingredient is the sounds of a cat's footsteps," I requested gracefully. She nodded and with a wave of her hands and a spell cast, she blessed the bonds with her cats' footsteps. The delicate ribbon then began to glow.

Njord was next through the doors, and I thought this was like an order decreed by the Norns. A master of the sea and seafaring came to my hall second, and the breath of a fish was the next ingredient. "King Njord, Fenrir's bonds need your magic. A breath of a fish is the next ingredient on the list," I said respectfully.

"Very well, let's get this over with, would be king," he replied, still feeling the effects of my previous dishonesty. He left to retrieve the breath from the sharks that pulled his chariot, returning moments later. With magical chants, a fish's breath was gifted to Gleipnir, allowing the dull glow to become brighter. It gave warmth to the cave where we gathered.

Heimdall came next to the council of gods. "Odin, the Draugr still roam in the realms. We require Vili's blade to keep them at bay." My mind had already found the solution for the Draugr, but I first needed Fenrir restrained.

"Brother, you have the vision of all realms, yes?" I asked. "We need to create a gateway for the dead. Fenrir is now at a colossal size, and I require mountains with deep roots to restrain his might." Heimdall stood tall, ever ready to aid me when I requested. "I need three mountains to secure Gleipnir to. He will become the ninth realm and home of all the Draugr,"

"And who will watch over the dishonourable dead?" Heimdall asked.

"Fenrir's sister. Hel is not comfortable in Asgard, and her home is in her brother's heart. In times of solitude sometimes the dead can provide company, with direction and purpose when contemplating their stories. She will be the queen of the dead and rule over them as such," I informed the three. "When Fenrir is bound, create a gateway to Niflheim just beyond the beast's jaws."

The fourth ingredient of the bonds made me ponder, considering the spittle of a bird sounded more like my abilities. I spat on Gleipnir, and the glow illuminated the entire room. Just then, Thor barged through the doors, sending my thoughts drifting towards the fifth ingredient. "The beard of a woman," I pondered while I stroked my beard.

"He'sss barely got a beard, Odin. I've always thought of him as a young woman," Loki chuckled while insulting Thor.

"Perhaps I should break your bones Loki," Thor snarled back.

"Silence!" I yelled, as my head began to cause me great pain. It ached so much when my visions of the future came to me. In this one, Thor was wearing a bridal gown next to Loki, while Loki was dressed as a maid.

Confused, I reached towards Thor and plucked a hair from his chin. After placing it on the fetters, it glowed so brightly, that it radiated the entire room. The glow was like a beacon of hope in the darkest of shadows.

Finally, through the doors, king Ullr arrived with Hel. I began to fear what the meaning behind the sixth ingredient was. The sinews of a bear, and here Ullr walked in his berserker attire. A tear rolled down my cheek as my mind cast back to Fenrir's warning of the next attempt to trap him.

Fenrir required a sign of good faith from his former friend and ally. It wasn't what I wished for, but it was the requirement to control such a massive beast. "Ullr, my son," I said hesitantly. "When the time comes, Fenrir will ask you for a gesture of goodwill. This gesture will change who you are forever, boy. You will become greater, and every being will respect you even more than they respect me. You will be the liaison between the Jotuns and the gods that wish to live in peace," I reassured the bear king with a heavy heart. Ullr was taken back for a few moments, but he was a brave king and knew what had to be done.

Suddenly, a great shadow was over the kingdom of the gods. A booming howl called us forth for his third and final challenge. "Evening, tiny gods," the wolf growled. "What challenge do you have for me today?" He asked just as confidently as he had in his previous victories. I revealed the glowing silk ribbon to the wolf, causing him to laugh. "There is no glory in breaking such little fetters. Do you gods think so little of me? Unless there is trickery in this attempt Odin?" he snarled with hatred in his eyes.

"These bonds can't hold you, Fenrir. You should disregard this attempt if you fear trickery," I teased.

"If you wish to trap me, I will ask for a gesture of goodwill. Perhaps my old friend would be so kind as to place a hand in my mouth. If I cannot break free and you do not release me, Ullr's hand will be his no longer." Ullr stepped forward bravely.

"I am unafraid of what is required, old friend. No sacrifice, no glory!" He yelled with chest puffed out. The wolf grinned sinisterly accepting his old friend's oath unaware of his limitless courage. Everything was unravelling according to plan but we needed him to be situated far from Asgard so the Draugr could not interfere with the residents of the gods.

The wolf and the gods left Asgard together and journeyed to Nepal. They were a peaceful people and very hardy, existing on only what they need and are enlightened to know when enough is enough. We then reached the mountains in Tibet with Fenrir, his shadow eclipsing the sun and casting darkness over the noble people. That place would be his prison. There he would remain secured to neighbouring mountains until Ragnarök.

Fenrir stood tall, looking down at all the gods, Loki included. They wrapped the constraints around the colossal beast's legs tightly. Ullr walked up to his old friend and stabbed the ground with one of his blades, then climbed the titan to get to his level. He had a great experience climbing this terrain growing up in Jotunheim and his expertise showed. Once Ullr reached the top, he placed his hand in the beast's mouth.

I looked around for confirmation from everyone securing the beast. The wolf smelled treachery in the air. "Ok mighty Fenrir Lokison. You may begin," I instructed while stepping back. Fenrir stretched and pulled using every ounce of his strength. Ullr flew through the air while his friend bit firmly enough to not ensure Ullr's hand remained in his mouth. As the wild wolf became a domesticated dog, his eyes burned with thoughts of revenge.

Freya's old magic began climbing up the legs of the wolf. Slowly, it crept higher. Flesh and fur became earth and stone. The wolf became stuck, quickly realising that this was it - this place was going to be his prison for a long time. Fenrir snapped his jaws shut as he bit down when he learned of the betrayal. We cheered in victory while Ullr's face held a series of emotions: regret for his betrayal of an old friend and the sadness and pain of losing his hand. He remained quiet. No sound of pain left his mouth. He held his bloodied stump as he turned his back and walked away slowly from his friend.

Fenrir's head stretched and struggled as his entire body was becoming the largest mountain in the world. While the gods rejoiced, I noticed the fire in Fenrir's eyes towards Ullr. The dog attempted to stretch just enough to claim the rest of Ullr. Luckily, I remained alert to snatch him away from the jaws of death.

"Tricky little gods. Release me now, and I'll send you all quickly," Fenrir vowed. Unafraid, I confronted the troublesome monster.

"If you don't have anything nice to say, Garmr. Perhaps you should remain silent," I declared. I grabbed Ullr's sword and plucked it from the ground, then stabbed him through his jaw, moments before he was consumed entirely by stone, he let out a harrowing howl that heralded the Draugr from all corners of the world. Together, we gods then created Helheim from his massive form. The howl beaconed the dead throughout every realm, causing them to flood to Fenrir's prison from all directions. Heimdall quickly used his magic to create a portal to Niflheim.

Niflheim is now Antarctica, but the veil made by Heimdall allows the dead to exist in comfort while not affecting those that are living.

Hel stepped forward from the crowd as the jaws of the massive beast became the gates to the realm of the dead. "This is yours, girl. My gift to you is a realm where the Draugr will remain, and you will call home," I said to her.

"My dinner table will welcome all. My bowl will be called hunger, my knife famine. My bed will be sickbed, and my blanket will be death," she replied.

"You will have my respect as an equal, Hel, the queen of Helheim," I said as she entered her realm.

Ullr looked at the blood pool created by his stump and called Eir, the mighty Valkyrie, to tend his wound. His thoughts drifted to his old companion trapped and regret continued to fill his heart as a single tear rolled down his cheek. I handed him my shield with adjustments made. "The lame can ride a horse, the handless drive cattle, the deaf can fight and prevail, it is happier to be blind than burning on the fire. An injury doesn't make you as useless as a corpse," I said to him with my hand on his shoulder. "You will now be known as Tyr, the god of war, justice and bravery. Your sacrifice for the realms is great and all shall respect your greatness," I declared, proud of the god my son had become.

# Gathering of Friends and Family

All was well in the worlds, and the nine realms were complete, but the sun and the moon began to slow. Day merged with night, and time stood still. Such an unnatural time was upon the worlds, and no rest or work would be completed. No crops would grow, no winds would blow. I called the council of gods to Urd's well. My lady came first, a testament to her everlasting loyalty was always much appreciated.

She entered with her small child she conceived with Njord. "Ah, young Freyr looks like a strong boy, my lady. Njord should be proud of his heir." Njord came to the table while I praised his offspring, still wary of me.

"Of course, I'm proud, king of gods. He will be a mighty leader one day. What solution do you have for our current troubles, oh wise leader?" He asked in a mocking tone.

When you obtain control of a group, you must remain cautious. Another might desire what you have, like a coiled snake preparing to strike. I must endure the cold and dark times. I must listen to my partner's pillow talk and watch for a broad sword slashing. A bear already played king once, and the eyes of my oath brother, Loki, would also be a threat.

The rest of the gods entered shortly after. Freya and Freyr sat to my right. Njord and Tyr to my left, across the table Heimdall, Sif and Thor. There was a ninth seat empty, reserved for Baldur's return. "Loki, you may hold this seat for a while. Your word will hold weight among the gods and your council will be respected. Your sly and cunning ways will prove useful in the times to come. Do all agree with this?" I asked the gods, scanning for a response, but all remained quiet.

"I agree," Heimdall answered.

"I agree," Freya spoke while nursing Freyr. Before long, the council agreed, and we began to discuss our current troubles.

"Two children in Alfheim exist, brother," Heimdall spoke first.

"And what can you tell me of these elves," I replied.

"They are beautiful and bright with the fight as ferocious as your Freya. Or so says their parents, my king." This angered Freya that the very ground shuddered beneath us.

"Ease yourself, my lady. The worlds know how you feel. Perhaps their roles will appease you, Freya," I said lovingly to reassure her of my care.

"Perhapsssss you should cast them on chariotsssss and have them pull the sssun and moon across the skiessss," Loki suggested in humour.

"Not a bad idea that'll ensure the celestial bodies will move and time will go on," I said, smiling at Loki's wit.

"What if they get tired and lose motivation, Odin? What then?" Njord asked, providing a problem to our solution.

"It's a matter of life and death of all realms of they remain slow or still," I warned the council.

The two hairs from my pocket that Verdandi stole from me created two giant wolves. These wolves would run across the skies in pursuit of the celestial bodies. If they were to remain still for too long, the prophecy of Ragnarök would come to pass quicker than I intend to allow it. "I had two hairs were from Tyr's attempts to trap Fenrir, but they were taken from me. The chain he made a mockery of and the other that inspired the beast to hate his handler. Verdandi intends to cast them in the air and give them form. Skoll and Hati will chase these elves in their duty. Send someone to collect these elves," I declared.

A short time had passed before Loki entered with the two elves. "Sol and Mani, your boasting of your beauty and talent are renowned, but I have a task for either of you. One must bring the sun and the other the moon," I said to both giving them great responsibility.

"Why should we?" they both asked.

"An honourable question, good elves. Life and death hang in the balance, with the sun and moon at a standstill. No nature will grow, and they your cargo is destined to be devoured, and war will follow. Death will come for everyone. Every god, elf and mortal alike. If you take up this honourable task, you will have days named after you in your honour, and everyone will respect you from now and even beyond Ragnarök. Sol's day and Mani's day," I declared to all in the realms on that day.

The elves agreed to take up the role, and their horses gifted to them were called, Hrimfaxi the frost mane. Hrimfaxi's drool fell on Midgard while Hati pursued on the long nights in winter. Sol's horses named Arvak and Alsvinn provided more pace along the sky. The dreaded Skoll would never be able to catch Sol, as I wanted to delay the prophecy of Ragnarök for as long as I could. She was promised to the giant eagle Suttung. He caused the winds of the world, and his marriage was thwarted. I never realised until all was too late, but Sol seemed pleased to avoid the Jotun king's advances.

So came the start of the naming of the days. Tyr was granted Tuesday, and Thor was gifted Thursday. My lady, that I loved so much, was given Friday, and my day, Wednesday, sat amongst them all. Saturday was a tribute to the one that allowed it all to happen. This was Ymir, the one that the Romans called Saturn. If it weren't for his death, life would never have been, and monsters would run throughout the dark void of the distant memory of Ginnungagap.

The roles of the council of gods were simple: they had to watch over each of the nine realms. Heimdall would be our brother's keeper as Farbauti furiously bashed more iron to create the sword that would eventually cause so much damage to my heart and the world during Ragnarök. Tyr would keep the peace in Jotunheim with his foster father's support. Thor would protect the humans in Midgard from any Jotun that dared harm the realm's residents. Freya would hold the dwarves' loyalty from her place in Folkvangr. Those creatures admired things of incredible beauty, and my lady's eyes would be the judge of such things. Two beautiful jewels of Gnoss and Gersemi is the only precious stones that would compare to the eyes she had for me. Njord would grant those who honoured him at boatyards protection from his mother and father in Vanaheim. Alfheim would be ruled by Freyr when he came of age in another attempt to gain Njord's allegiance, but a sword of a king would be needed to anoint the position eventually.

My brother's old sword came to mind, but I'd have to regain Mimir's ring that was in possession of Fafnir. There would be only one in Midgard that I would trust to reclaim the ring and return it to me. Each of the gods spat into a bowl, myself included. Each spit held the wise words of each contributor, and with a bit of magic, we created a man—a man wise of head and heart. His name would be Kvasir, and he would be the wisest man in all of the realms. He was created to teach the mortals the ways of the gods. The council quickly dispersed from Urd's well and I left towards Midgard. I disguised myself as my son's wise uncle and spread the word that I knew the future. The bait was set, and it wasn't long before Sigurd appeared for council.

# Sigurd's Destiny

Do you know what Wyrd is? Destiny is a funny concept that some stumble across, and others require a nudge. Some fates are woven with others, and some divert away for a time only to return at a later date. Sigurd's destiny needed a push. He had to return to Asgard one day to reunite with his brothers and sisters; to reunite with his mother and me. He was a king worthy of ascension to Asgard, and perhaps when my time is over, he could replace me. However, the problem with being a god is that you can't just outright claim divinity. Rulership over mortals was never my desire. They were like us, albeit a shorter lifespan, but we all had to find our path up our own mountains.

Disguised as a distant uncle, I requested Sigurd's presence. I had a prophecy to share with him. Sigurd had travelled far but desired to know more of his saga from the future. He entered the hall of his unknown uncle. "Uncle Merlin, I have come far with word that Skuld whispers in your ear," Sigurd announced.

"I long for her whispers more, nephew. What do you seek?" I asked.

"What has been decreed by the Norns for me?" The noble king asked.

"Well, nephew, your fate will require a price, a price that only you can pay, boy," I said.

"Name it," he replied eagerly.

"Your fate will be to go home, your real home amongst brothers and sisters of equal greatness. Everything dies, good Sigurd. You must go out seeking what you desire. Asgard awaits your glorious return, boy. Everything dies, but your name is fated to live on through your great accomplishments. Your exploits will make you the most loved by men, Jotun and elf. All realms will respect you, and all women will desire you. This is your wyrd, my nephew." Sigurd was taken back with my words. He stood in shock. "Be warned, Sigurd Odinson, your triumph will be your doom. The dwarves used to have much but now have nothing. Fools and their money are easily parted. Teach Fafnir that riches are the falsest of friends, especially as the foolish Fafnir grows more arrogant with his wealth. His arrogance grows, not his wisdom. Seek out Regin. His brother holds the payment I require for the revelation of your fate. Regin will grant you the tools required to defeat his brother and gain the ring I require."

Sigurd left on his mighty white horse to seek out the crafty Regin. He rode hard toward his destination, keen to fulfil my requested payment through blistering winds, bone-chilling winters and scorching summer days. After three years of travel, he found himself at Regin's forge. After following every lead, his quest was only beginning. "Dwarf, I have ridden for some time. I was told that you would have the tools to defeat your brother," Sigurd declared to the twisted little dwarf.

"That I do, boy, but only those that are higher born may be able to defeat the terror that is my brother. Tell me of your father?" Regin inquired.

"I am a descendant of Odin, the king of the gods. There are none higher born than I, dwarf," Sigurd replied. "I must slay your brother to return home with honour to Asgard. Where are the items for this task?" Regin's eyes widened at the thought someone had finally come, after all these years, which could defeat his brother.

The two went beyond the front of the forge to gain the first of three tools to defeat the mighty dragon. Regin peeled back a curtain to reveal an enchanted blade encased in stone. "This sword, the scale piercer, is my brother's old blade. The goddess Freya placed it there. She claimed it would remain in the stone until one of her blood removed it. Excalibur will cut any foe down," Regin boasted as Sigurd grabbed its handle to free it from its stone holster. While Sigurd's hand grasped the hilt, the blade began to emanate an immense power around the forge. Sigurd pulled it swiftly from its prison, slicing the stone cleanly in two.

Regin led him to a chest that revealed protection from everything. "This helmet of awe will protect you from all threats. It was Freya that requested it to be built. Nothing in the nine realms can harm you while wearing this magnificent item," Regin gloated while calculating his plot.

"What is the marking inscribed?" Sigurd asked curiously.

"Why that marking is Ægishjálmr. It is a rune from Freya herself. The legend says she travelled the worlds getting oaths from everything. These oaths would protect the wearer of the helmet from all harm. The third item you require is knowledge, son of Odin. Fafnir lies hoarding his riches in the caves of the great mountains. If you challenged him there, it would be suicide. Many have held their breath to avoid his toxic nature and his venom had seeped through many a brave warrior's pores. Patience will be your greatest ally when slaying my brother, young man. Take this map it'll guide you to him. All I request, Sigurd, is for you to cook my brother's heart and share a meal with me." Sigurd agreed, keen to rejoin his brothers in Asgard when all is finished.

Sigurd left with Excalibur by his side and the helm of awe atop his head. Between Regin's and his uncle's advice, he was racing bravely towards his destiny. Unknown to him, I was in pursuit as a raven, soaring high above the clouds and far enough out of sight to not raise suspicion.

# Dragon Slayer

Sigurd galloped rapidly to Fafnir's territory. He pulled his beautiful white steed to secure him to a tree unaffected by the toxic air. Proceeding on foot towards a sizeable leafless tree with a view of Fafnir's cave, the day became dark and gloomy with the stench of death filling the air. Sigurd decided to put his helmet on to protect him from the effects of the foul stench. As he got closer, the corpses of fallen heroes littered the path. The day crept slowly into the night, as the darkness came over the land. The silence was replaced with the sound of rocks falling from the mountain, creating an uneasy feeling in brave Sigurd. A beast stirred from within his cave. Sigurd climbed up to hide in the thick, dense branches of the dead tree. It gave him a great scouting advantage, being able to view a large area from above. The tree was too brittle to support something of great size, so he figured he would be safe there if his presence was not detected.

A deep groan came from within the dark cave, as the mountain trembled at what stirred within. A terrifying sight emerged: a beast with massive claws and fangs dripping venomous drool. Sigurd perched high in the tree, watching the reptile slither down the side of the rocky cliffs. When it reached the foot of the mountain, it slipped beneath the foliage of the forest. The trees bent as the serpent crawled through them. The thuds became squelches when it reached the marshes. Breaking through the tall grass, he emerged at the river to quench his thirst.

The stench was foul and intensified the closer the hideous creature came. Through the noise of the beast's movements, Sigurd could hear the sounds of ravens cawing in the distance filling the deathly silence. Sigurd grasped tightly to Excalibur's handle as the dragon passed below, but he recalled Regin's advice. He tried to remain as still as possible as he viewed the giant dragon quench his thirst from the stream. "Is that Fafnir? The dwarf?" He thought to himself.

As Fafnir finished his drink, he smelled something in the air and scanned the area for movement. Sigurd made sure not to move a muscle to alert the dragon of his presence. He held his breath while Fafnir continued to sniff the air.

One of the fallen heroes coughed and spat up blood near the bank. His corpse was torn and ravaged by the dragon, but still, he bravely held onto life by a thread. Fafnir heard the cough and slithered toward its source. He found the hero, and in one swift bite, consumed what remained. Sigurd watched on regretfully as the dragon finished his meal before following the same path, he took down the mountain to return to his cave.

Sigurd remained in the tree until morning. A gloomy overcast hovered above. He didn't want to disturb the landscape but needed to do something. He then considered masking his scent from the beast he was monitoring. He decided to cover himself in mud from head to toe from the dwelling of the dead heroes accumulated by the mighty dragon. He draped fresh bones around his neck with the maggots crawling over the undigested flesh. The stench of death would do well to camouflage the aroma of his scent.

He used twigs and sticks as markers throughout the dragon's trail to gain a more accurate location of its path. Once finished and as the sun began to set on the horizon, a bleak day slowly slipped into the night. Sigurd quickly made his way back to his tree before the dragon made his way for a drink once more.

The grumbling mountains wailed as Fafnir woke again. The beast proceeded down the ridge following the same path, a creature of habit, through the dead trees in the forest. He slid through the marshes of corpses, then beast broke through the tall grass slithering down to the stream. The stench of death masked his odour, and after Fafnir's thirst was satisfied, he returned home to his cave.

The following day when it was gloomy and overcast overhead once more, Sigurd departed from his tree to find an exact spot to execute both plan and beast. The twigs were mostly unbroken and undisturbed. He continued scanning, hopeful that at least one would provide a proper location. His eyes looked ahead and spotted the broken sticks in the marsh that had been shattered by Fafnir's steps, causing him to begin digging a hole in the exact location. He needed it to be deep enough to conceal him but narrow enough for the dragon to go over with ease. Covering it with grass, he lay in wait as the sun began to set. Darkness overcame the land on the third night as Mani pulled the moon across the night sky. The glow from it lit up the terrain that provided comfort to the hero's courage.

As he lay in wait, the familiar sound came from the mountain. The rocks tumbled down into the forest's edge. The trees creaked as they gave way to the giant hero killer. The ground trembled in anticipation, for her son lay hidden from vision. Each step of the beast became stronger and stronger, and Sigurd's back felt every vibration. The stench of the beast became overwhelming causing his grip to tighten on his sword.

It was nearly time. He looked up at the moon as Hati howled in the distance and readied himself, waiting for the opportune moment. In an instant, Mani's bright glow vanished into darkness as the dragon crawled over the trap. Sigurd bravely plunged his sword upward through Fafnir's chest and deep into his heart. Fafnir roared so violently that ravens took off calling in the distance. Regin heard the roar and began to journey to the source at once.

Fafnir thrashed hard in his final moments only to lay by the stream he visited frequently. As Sigurd emerged from the hole, the tail of the dragon whipped the hero, sending him flying into a tree, but the helmet he wore provided him protection from all harm. Sigurd rose to his feet, where he stood safely, and waited till the beast's thrashing came to an end. He marched slowly towards his fallen foe, he plunged his sword deep in his adversary's chest, before he claimed his prize.

Sigurd took his helmet off, placing it at his side, and used his blade to carve the heart from the dragon's breast. He then made a fire to cook the meat to Regin's request. Testing the heart too soon, he burned his finger, automatically putting it in his mouth to numb the pain. Regin approached and I landed near my son's camp at the same time. With the dragon's blood he consumed when he burned his finger, he could now understand me in the form of a bird.

Dragons have always been a source of mystery and wonder over the millennia. The hold wisdom where none dare to go. They contain a magic unlike any other tied to ferocity and the hoarding of gold. A serpent that can fly will always understand the songs of the birds.
"Regin approaches king Sigurd," I warned. "He wants Fafnir's ring that you promised to another. He will kill you for it, too," I cawed before flying off.

"Ah, young Sigurd, you did it," Regin said, appearing from behind the trees with Sigurd's steed.

"Why do you have my horse? I have begun to cook the meat you requested. I'm sure it won't take long," Sigurd said, turning his back to Regin to go fetch water for the feast. As he bent down to collect it, Regin crept up behind with dagger in hand, but the moonlight revealed Regin's reflection in the water, alerting Sigurd of the dwarf's plan. The dwarf rushed to stab Sigurd, only for Sigurd to turn and plunge his blade deep into Regin's chest.

Blood flowed from the wound and mixed with Fafnir's. The Hreidmar line had ended, and Sigurd got his hands on the magical sack that contained Andalfari's treasure. The dragon's death brought life to the land again, later causing the world to have great respect for Sigurd once all had heard of his success.

Noble Sigurd kept his word returning the ring to me and all in the nine realms celebrated his victory. Such fame gained him respect from all kingdoms, even those twisted in nature. However, it is best to find praise in yourself instead of relying on others for validation.

He would return home to live amongst the Aesir as Baldur one day, but unfortunately, his adventure was not over yet. Unknown to him, the blood of the Hreidmar line provided fertiliser for a new plant to emerge. Young and innocent, it had not taken the oath that blessed his helmet. This plant was mistletoe, and sure enough, his glory would eventually lead to his doom.

With Fafnir's death, Nidhoggr's spirit was released from the ring. The spirit drifted to the root of the world tree beneath Helheim, where it would be trapped, waiting for his time to strike. There he would remain to gnaw at the tree's root slowly and if any twisted spirits were to be so unlucky to cross his path, they would be consumed at a moment's notice. After their consumption, they would find themselves in Farbauti's realm where he was building his army to attack the home of the gods. Ragnarök was on its way.

# Love and Hate

Mani and Hrimfaxi galloped hard and fast across the skies and Hati fell for the celestial body. A colossal wolf ran over the land and water forever in pursuit of the one that was out of reach. Her longing could be heard from time to time with howls towards the love that will never be hers.

As I sat by the fire with the ring in hand, I realised that one couldn't understand love without hate as a comparison. Peace with Njord was the ultimate goal as it would bring me closer to Freya's hand in marriage and make the Aesir and Vanir stronger through the union. I retired that night with thoughts of my lady but also thoughts on the future ruler of the elves.

The next day, Sol's chariot pulled the sun across the blue sky, I continued my journey to Mimir's well. The population of Jotuns soared with the removal of Draugr and most could be avoided or tricked to let a humble old man pass. Trolls desired trinkets of gold and silver, ogres valued food and drink; giants liked to play games and prove their superiority, among others. Each had a weakness that any wise man could exploit.

I approached my uncle's well while an eagle flew high above. This great eagle was Suttung, the Jotun king, the greatest Jotun of all. He cast a great shadow over me as he watched amongst the clouds. He longed for his wife, Sol, placed high above where he could fly. He was the master of the winds, wise and powerful, and noble of purpose. As a leader, he had my respect, but as an enemy, he had my focus.

I entered Mimir's cave, where my uncle's head was being served a drink by a boy that was very familiar to me. Although I did not yet know his name, I felt drawn to him. Mimir finished his drink, and the boy wiped his face before leaving the room. "Uncle, nice to see you again," I said.

"Never mind the pleasantries. what do you want?" Mimir asked.

"I have come to return Vili's gift, uncle," I said, placing the ring by his head.

"Give it to your boy. He has a hand to wear it," he said with a smirk.

"My boy?" I curiously asked as there was more than one.

"The boy who aids me is young Vidar. He is your son from the time you spent in Jotunheim so long ago," Mimir informed me. "Since you returned the ring, I will give you Vili's sword and two other gifts, nephew," Mimir said as two white ravens flew in the entrance to land on my shoulders.

"Huginn and Muninn," I said after hearing their calls as they flew in. My companions, my scouts and my allies on the throne. Their white feathers glistened in the light as a symbol of purity. That would change as the truth is rarely so innocent.

I thanked my uncle as I left to head back to Asgard and inform the rest of the gods of my decision on the ruling of Vanaheim.

Suddenly, the winds became gales. These powerful winds would knock most mortals to the floor, but I braced myself with my spear, ready for a battle. When the giant eagle hovering above swooped down and landed in front of me, I was on guard was ready. "Odin, why did you take her? Why did you take my wife?" Suttung asked.

"Suttung, nice to finally meet you. Apologies, but it was your wife's choice to take up the task. I'm sorry for your loss, friend. There were no other options." He became furious with scepticism at the truth of my words.

"What do you seek more than a woman's love and touch?" Suttung asked, probing for weaknesses.

"Knowledge and wisdom, and enough time to obtain both," I replied in haste to make a natural ally of him. It was unfortunate that Suttung's revenge consumed his thoughts.

"I will hurt you where it hurts most, Allfather," he vowed before flying off, causing the great winds to stir once more.

I made it hastily back to Asgard and called for the council to convene once more. Freyr was a toddler now cracking his first tooth. He was such a handsome little boy. My Freya was beautiful with her green eyes and flowing red locks. She was beauty and power personified. She's even nursed Freyr closely as a young boy. Sometimes they'd share a bed.

As the other gods entered my hall, one by one, I welcomed and sat each at the table.  Each god quickly declared their issues and had heated discussions—concerns with Jotuns, the twisted nature of some dwarves and the appointment of leadership to each realm.

"Now, the last issue to discuss is Alfheim's rule," The room was silent as they listened tentatively. Each of the gods was eager to claim multiple lands to rule. "Freyr, Njord's son, will rule over the elves. He is noble of lineage and will be a mighty king," I announced and waited patiently for a response. The silence and stern looks filled the room. I was stunned as everyone agreed for the first time. Slowly, I earned Njord's respect and blessing to rule as king of the gods by declaring his son as ruler of the elves.

Freya would raise and train her female warriors. These Valkyrie determined the worth of the fallen to join and fight for a place among the Einherjar. Each warrior had to prove their place as my hall had its limits, and if they fell on the battlefield in Asgard, they made their way to Helheim. Freya commanded legions of Valkyries, and I had the greatest of warriors from all lands join me. Our forces would continue to grow and renew until Heimdall blew on the Gjallarhorn.

As I retired to my seat to watch over the nine realms, Suttung drew the focus of my thoughts. I wronged him in such a way that left me regretful with my actions, but what was done could not be undone. My all-seeing eye looked to Midgard and spotted Kvasir the wise. He wandered around Midgard, teaching all who crossed his path. His fame grew amongst the mortals, but popularity always comes at a price. Being good to some will damage relations with others and by scouting the different lands, Huginn and Muninn learned the truth of this and became a little darker in colour.

# In the Shadows

This part of the tale is even more twisted than most. It served a lesson that no matter how good your intentions, others may still want the worst for you regardless.

The two goblins Verdandi transformed travelled through Midgard under cover of darkness. They lived in solitude in the shadows of thick trees in the forest at the edge of Sigurd's kingdom that provided shade and shelter. The locals would rarely see them, and if they did, they would be fortunate if they survived an encounter.

Their features caused fear and panic, that even the mere mentioning of them would cause one to lose sleep. With skin pale as a corpse, eyes tinged yellow with their desires for blood, wrinkled skin with hunched backs, they were as twisted in form as they were in nature. The brothers feasted on the rotten carcasses of dead animals near their forest-dwelling. Sometimes, hidden in the shadows, when no moonlight shone, they would venture out to nearby castles to observe the nobles and gain inspiration for their creations. Although twisted, these short beings had a talent for creating things of great power and beauty.

One such night happened to cause Fjalar and Galar, the goblins that were twisted by Verdandi's magic, to leave the forest on their mission to pursue Verdandi's desires for revenge. Clouds blotted out the moon's glow and not a star appeared in the sky. They approached the nearby town staying in the shadows that the flicker of the town's torches cast. They crept to the harbours underneath the boardwalks, and from behind some crates, they were taken by the beauty of how well the boats before them were built. Grunting and snorting on their way, the locals that overheard them dismissed them thinking they were wild pigs looking for scraps.

The next place they visited was the blacksmith's forge. They peered through the minor cracks in the walls as their yellow eyes focused on the awe and abilities of the human forges. There were spear tips, heavy axes and strong shields, each item useful and created with care. The clinks and clanks of the blacksmith's hammer lit up the room with each blow. Consumed by the beauty of it all, Fjalar let out an "ooooh." The blacksmith paused, scanning around for the source. Galar thought quickly to imitate an owl.

"It's late. I'd better head to bed soon," the blacksmith reassured himself.

He grasped the long handle of his hammer and began to work the metal again as eyes watched on once more in awe. Blow after blow, the dwarves' grins widened once more causing them to salivate at the mouth. Clink, clink crunch!

"Good gods!" The blacksmith yelled out of frustration as the head of his hammer broke causing him to throw the remainder of it at the wall. This caused the brothers to realise why there were cracks in the walls to peek through. Their grins fell from their hideous and grotesque faces at the thought of being discovered, so they continued to scout out the area.

Confident with their lack of detection, the brothers decided to head to the castle. Each entrance had guards posted and some patrolled the courtyard. The brothers revelled in the challenge, though, as they climbed a wall quicker and more silently than a spider. They leapt high and fast, maintaining their stealth in the cover of darkness. Their moves were so quick that Heimdall could only detect the faintest of whistles. They both hurried up the castle wall until they reached the feasting hall.

Sigurd was informing his kin of how he slew the mighty Fafnir, gesturing every swing of Excalibur with his dinner knife. All cheered and celebrated his success as he boasted of the fate of Fafnir and Regin. The brothers screwed up their already twisted faces at the news of the death of their kin but did not make plans for revenge as they knew they could not harm him.

"….and then Regin fell to my blade. That'll teach him for trying to kill me!" Sigurd's voice boomed around the hall while the generals listened.

"SKÅL!" One of the warriors announced as he raised his horn. Each of the kin around the circular table followed after.

The feasting continued when one knight asked, "And what of tomorrow, my king? Any more dragons to slay?" Sigurd smiled in response.

"If I were to slay all the dragons, what glory would be left for the rest of you?" Sigurd replied to the attempt to mock him. "No, I await one created by the gods. He is wise and educated. He contains the wisdom of all the gods combined. He possesses the logic from the Aesir and the passion of the Vanir. He will know the way I must go to return to Asgard. Kvasir journeys now through the forests at the edge of the kingdom. He should be here tomorrow evening," Sigurd said enthusiastically.

Fjalar and Galar looked at each other with thoughts of evil plans. Distracted with their thoughts, one of the patrol guards yelled up from the courtyard. "At the window!" Sigurd stood up from his chair frozen in shock.

Two sets of eyes stared back at him. Glowing yellow, they looked like the eyes of death that held much hardship to the beloved warrior. Those glowing, yellow eyes were Verdandi's, and they would haunt the hero in times to come.

Immediately, those gathered began to fire their arrows, watching the brothers hurrying retreat. They made it back to their forest home quickly and began to feel relieved knowing they were safe in the shadows were none dared to enter due to the fear and mystery there.

The brothers then began plotting revenge and the interception of the wise traveller that was making his journey towards Sigurd. They wished to boast and celebrate their victory over Sigurd the same way he rejoiced in the slaying of Fafnir and Regin. They constructed three vats that they called Óðrœrir, Boðn and Són. These three vats would be essential to executing their plan.

# Quenching a Thirst

Huginn and Muninn were soaring high above collecting information that my all-seeing eye couldn't gather from Hlidskjalf. They kept watchful eyes on the one created from the union of both godly tribes. Gliding on the winds, they landed only to gather enough information for me to decide on whether to act.

Meanwhile, the weary traveller had wandered through towns and cities through the years, stopping at any residence that provided accommodation. Kvasir was old and sprinkled with the salt and bitterness of wisdom throughout his head and face. He would always share the tales of travel and wisdom, combining the head and heart in his teachings. The wisdom and logic but also the empathy it takes to know what to share with those who seek his council. This gained much respect throughout Midgard.

Even Aegir and Ran accepted Kvasir for a while. With them, he learned about Ran's net, among many other fascinating things. Kvasir was neither Aesir nor Vanir but contained the best of both.

He hiked through the large forest, pushing past the tree branches, clearing his path as the route became denser and absent of light. Sunlight could not reach this part of the forest. As the rich green leaves became fewer in number, their empty branches began wounding him. They shredded his arms, as he braced himself on a dead and hollow branch that gave way. The twigs sliced open his hand, and the scent of his blood drifted across the forest to the Strigoi.

As Fjalar and Galar finished their empty containers for mead, smelling the sweet scent of blood in the air. They scampered towards their objective with haste, drooling on their way. They were wretched creatures jumping from tree to tree, swiftly closing in on their prey.

Kvasir paused for only a moment to wrap his hand. The wind was still aside the sound of Huginn and Muninn cawing that left an eerie feeling in the curious wanderer. It was like a warning of what was coming his way. A stick snapped in the trees above as the two Strigoi hunted their prey.

"Show yourself!" Kvasir yelled into the air. No one responded, but as he turned, Galar appeared from behind the tree. "Hideous creatures, what do you want?"

"Ah, wise one, you do not know? But you know all. Maybe you aren't the one Sigurd seeks," Galar suggested. Fjalar appeared from behind a different tree.

"So sweet the smell. You are either of great wisdom or foolishness to enter these woods," Fjalar stated.

"I'm Kvasir, the wisest of men, and I do not suffer fools," Kvasir warned while drawing his knife and raising it towards these dark elves.

"Easy Kvasir, we want no trouble here. We simply want to give you rest to tend to your wounds and give you a feast," Fjalar said reassuringly.

"Yes, no trouble here. We only require a test of your legendary wisdom. Follow us back to our home, and we can guide you to Sigurd's castle," Galar said.

Kvasir holstered his blade, but his wits were sharper, and he was keen to keep them at the forefront of his mind should anything go wrong. The twisted brothers directed him to an easier path in the woods that led him to their dwellings. As he crossed the threshold, he looked left and right, scanning for possible threats. Taking a seat, he remained suspicious of those twisted little creatures, as he was still uncertain if either were foe or friend.

"What wisdom do you desire?" Kvasir asked after he sat at the table. He should have given courteous silence instead of being bold. His ears should've remained attentive, and his eyes alert so that he remained protected.

"Legend speaks that you have come from the Aesir and Vanir," Galar mentioned.

"So, you would know the way back, right?" Fjalar interrupted eagerly.

"I have been gifted praise and wisdom for what you seek. So honoured I am to receive such...." Fjalar stopped him mid-sentence.

"Brother, grab the wine and fill our guest's cup." Galar left and opened the door to the kitchen, revealing three large vats. A cold shiver ran up Kvasir's spine as he began to discover the true intentions of his hosts. Galar returned with wine while Kvasir's grip tightened on his knife under the table.

After a few harmless questions followed by a few respectful words, Kvasir's guard dropped. They began to share the wine throughout the day and had many discussions. Kvasir revealed the way to Asgard but returned with his questions as he became inebriated. "What are the containers for in the kitchen?" He asked while hiccupping.

"You'll find out soon enough," Galar said, smirking.

"Ah, I forgot the time. Sigurd awaits my arrival," Kvasir said. Trying to rise out of his seat, he fell back into his chair. His legs and arms were no longer under his control. Paralysed, the brothers moved closer, as their eyes became a murky yellow and their teeth became sharpened fangs.

Fjalar bit down on Kvasir's jugular vein on the left side of his neck while Galar prepared the drip trays beneath Kvasir's chair before clamping his jaws on the right side. Drunk Kvasir got, dead drunk when he was seated with Fjalar the wise. Best is the feast that you live through only to recall all that happened.

As Kvasir's lifeless body twitched in his seat, the brothers emptied his blood into the three vats. His body was now a drained vessel with dread on its face. "We got what we wanted," Galar told his brother.

"And now we are taking what we need," Fjalar said in reply.

As the last of the blood was harvested from the throat, the Strigoi filled the Vat Óðrœrir with the blood. Due to the unique origin of Kvasir's blood, they became thirsty to spill even more. With each sip of it, their forms became altered into more human-like appearances, but smaller in stature. They became sophisticated and strong as they shed their grotesque looks. This blood caused them to become more creative in their hunt. Once they realised, they would never stalk their prey anymore. They would simply invite them to feast.

After their intoxication of Kvasir's blood, the vampiric brothers decided they required more blood to sustain them. They sent an invitation to a Jotun king and his wife with the intention of filling the other two Vats.

Huginn and Muninn returned to me almost entirely black. Such horrors for Midgard. Who could blame them for being tainted by the darkness? I sent the ravens back to Midgard to inform Sigurd of Kvasir's fate given that was his only chance to return home.

The sons of Verdandi knew Sigurd's way to Asgard, but he'd have to gain their favour first as they could aid him in his journey. Now that there is peace between the tribes of gods, Sigurd had to earn his way back to Asgard and become Baldur once more.

After my exchange with Huginn and Muninn, I collected Kvasir's body from a shallow unmarked grave in the forest. The brothers remained unaware of my presence, as I walked that forest like a ghost, never leaving a trace of me ever being there. I was as subtle as a breeze in the darkness. My faint whistles were dismissed as airflow through the unusual branches.

Carrying Kvasir's soulless corpse to Asgard, I hoped to reunite him with what was taken. Little did I know this would change me and those that share my table in Valhöll.

# Blood is Thicker than Water

The brothers sent an invitation to Jotunheim. The king and queen, Gilling and his wife, were invited to the eerie woods far away on the border of Svartalfheim and Midgard. Tyr had advised against it, but his words fell on deaf ears as they left their two sons to rule in their stead.

While they were gone, Suttung and Baugi managed their kingdom. One worked on the throne and the other handled the kingdom's agriculture, ensuring all had enough to eat. Suttung ruled and longed for his lost love and plotted his revenge against the one who separated them.

In the wilderness, Gilling sang the most beautiful songs. He had a voice that boomed throughout the forest and that was as strong as his giant steps that made the ground tremble. His singing was an attempt to soothe his wife's distress on such a far journey. She wasn't used to travelling and the haunting sounds and the uneasiness of harsh leafless trees made her imagination fear the worst. The singing appeared to calm her even though the unknown dangers she feared were up ahead.

Through the trees, the mighty Jotun king went singing away, alerting all to his presence and allowing the sinister vampire brothers to hear them coming. It was then the dwarves decided to put their plans into action against the royal couple.

Unable to overpower the giant, they decided to confront the royals at a large body of water in the forest. They knew the royals would look for the quickest way to overcome the obstacle as they did not plan ahead to overcome the vastness. They quietly waited for them to arrive, once they had, the brothers watched as they surveyed the water.

Too far to swim and too vast to go around, the king and queen contemplated what to do next as the sun receded behind the horizon and the night consumed the day. They knew they needed to try to arrive before it was too late.
As they examined the lake, they could hear gentle splashes, but could not see where or who they were coming from. Unbeknownst to them, these noises were caused by the vampiric brothers and were the strokes of paddles in perfect rhythm. Appearing from the shadows, the brothers

masked their monstrous forms. "We can offer a ride to you, large people. One at a time, though, as our boat is small," Galar said under his hood.

"I'll go first. Wife, stay here by the fireside, and I will send them back for you," Gilling said bravely, unaware of the dangers he faced. After reassuring his wife, he left, oblivious that this would be the last journey he would ever take.

Hours later, the brothers returned to the queen, tired from their exploits. She boarded their boat, happy to be no longer alone. The crossing was eerily quiet, causing the queen to feel uncomfortable. "How is my husband?" she asked to fill the eery silence on the water.

"Heavy, my lady. He fell overboard," Fjalar said to the queen. Worry and fear chased across her face.

"Don't worry, we dragged him to shore and carried him to our place. He's resting there waiting for you to join him," Galar reassured. While the brothers tied their boat on the shore, the queen noticed drag marks on the path she assumed they had to take.

"Yes, these are your husbands, your Majesty. He was a deadweight after making it to shore, but not to worry, he rests now. He was pretty drained from his experience," Fjalar said, smirking sinisterly. This reassurance brought relief to the queen, causing her to continue to be blind to her husband's fate.

After a short journey, their home appeared through a clearing. Galar sauntered with the queen while Fjalar rushed ahead to prepare for their visitor. "You will be reunited soon, my lady," Galar said, comforting the queen as they approached and moved down the path.

When they finally arrived, Galar pushed the creaky door open and drew the queen's gaze for a moment. As she stepped through the threshold, her eyes looked ahead and revealed the horrors the brothers had done to her husband.

She should have checked her surroundings when entering a stranger's door. No one knows where friend, foe or danger may be.

Suddenly, her head flooded with pain following a loud bang. She immediately threw her hand to the place of impact and surprised with the warm rush of red fluid passing through her fingers. It was then she looked to the ground and noticed the large rock, which she assumed was the weapon. As her vision blurred, the dwarves watched her fall to the ground with a loud thud.

Slowly, the queen regained her senses. She found her world was turned upside down as she was now suspended from her ankles. Just below her head, she saw a vat labelled Boðn. To her right, the drained corpse of her husband also hung with a vat labelled Són below his head.

"Ah, you're awake. We told you we would reunite you both," Galar said, removing his hood. Fjalar used his red cap to mop the blood from the floor. It was then that realisation of what was going on became clear and too much to bear. She began to sob.

"Aaawwww boohoo," Fjalar mocked.

"Yeah, we are the ones that should be crying. We had to hall your husband's limp body back here," Galar said as he puffed. The sobbing became louder, much to the brothers' discomfort. Their eyes glowed yellow as they crept toward the Queen, watching her eyes widen in fear, as her impending death was fast approaching. They quickly sliced her throat and gleefully watched as Boðn filled to the brim. The Jotun royals were dead, reunited in the vats that contained their blood.

Aside from the transformation of appearance, the blood gave the vampiric brothers three unique ingredients for good poetry, songs or writings. These three ingredients were only found in these specific victims: wisdom, empathy and sorrow. With all three vats filled, they were mixed with sweet honey and brewed into the magical mead of poetry. Óðrœrir comprised passion to border the point of madness. Són encompassed melodies and rhythm like the beating of a heart. Boðn contained the sorrow and essence that caused listeners to feel the emotions behind the words spoken. Unknown to them, with each sip of Óðrœrir, the brothers became more inspired in creating tools and designing of weapons. With each drink of Boðn, sorrow and regret of their previous actions filled their hearts, and with every sip of Són, they sang of the dreaded fall of Kvasir, Gilling and his wife.

Those songs travelled far, floating on the very wind to reach the ears of a being that neither the brothers nor I would have liked.

I sent Huginn to tell Sigurd to set sail for an island. I even asked Njord to grant him swift travel to his destination. I desired that mead, as it would give me a magical ability I had yet to possess. The magickal mead would gift me with heightened senses that could assess the reactions to my words, how to inspire, manipulate and even drive women to love.

# Mysterious Stranger

Fjalar and Galar became more inspired with every mouthful of the mead they drank, causing them to steadily evolve. Their skin became paler as time went on. They were quick to move and freakishly strong. They still hunted, but less frequently. The one thing that did not change about them, was their preference of embracing the night under the cover of darkness and shadow. They rose to become the most elite predators in all the lands, thanks to being empowered by Verdandi and transformed by Jotun, Aesir and Vanir blood.

Closely related to the dwarves, building came naturally to them. Their newfound forms were empowered by the mead to construct a great new castle in a faraway land, away from their original habitat near Sigurd's castle. It took them nine nights to complete their home, but it hid from the sun in the day as it was a threat to them. They wished to keep Verdandi pleased by not aiding Sigurd's return to Asgard. Fjalar and Galar's castle had tall towers, large doors and few windows to keep Sol's cargo from ending their lives. Deep within the dungeons they created an outstanding forge. One brother would work the bellows and the other would use the heat from the forge to create great items to buy them favour from the locals and those from distant lands. One such item was a large kettle for brewing ale, along with a magically enchanted cup that was hard to break. Many magical items in the tales of the gods could be traced back to Fjalar and Galar, or their new identities called Brokkr and Eitri.

One night, they got so intoxicated they accidentally drank from the blood of Gilling. As a side effect, familiar words poured from their mouths in a dear tune, most beautiful and acquainted to some. Stumbling around their castle, they made it to the balcony on the highest tower and sang the song Gilling once had in order to soothe his wife's worries so long ago.

The night was peaceful, barely a breeze. The moon was at half its glory as the stars flickered like dancers' sequins on a dress. It was beautiful. The intimate song drifted through the night like a boat on the sea and floated on the wind unknown to all, except one.

The next night the brothers enjoyed some more of the sweet mead, as per usual, when booming knocks rattled and echoed throughout their castle. "Dinner?" Fjalar asked Galar.

"Another victim, brother. Let's savour and enjoy this one." In a flash, they were at the door as it creaked and was slowly opening to the stranger. His giant figure towered over them. They welcomed him, cautiously, intimidated by his frame.

"I'll take your cloak," Galar said politely, ushering him into their feast hall.

"Weary traveller, what is your name? What brings you to our doors?" Fjalar asked, guiding the man to his chair.

"I am Thyazi, and the winds guided me here," the man said as he warmed his hands near the flame.

Fjalar prepared a meal and a bottle of ale for the strange man. Once the dinner was laid before him, they began to probe him for more information. "What can you tell us of your family?" Galar wanted to find out if anyone would miss him after his death.

"My brother tends the farm at home, and my parents, well, they are what started my journey," Thyazi said, blowing into his cupped hands before rubbing them together. The night continued, and the brothers kept probing, but the man never revealed more than he needed.

Fjalar got up to fill his and his brother's cup with Gilling's blood. Taking a sip on his way back to the table, he hummed a tune, unaware that it was familiar to their guest.

"Nice tune," the man said to Fjalar. "My father used to sing to my brother and me a song like that on nights such as this," Thyazi rose from his seat.

The brothers were taken back by the guest's sudden movement. The chair flew back, and the winds from outside rushed into the hall. Thyazi clutched the two brothers in a furious rage and began to transform into something powerful.

The brothers struggled with all their might, but it was no match for the giant visitor. Their guest's hands were replaced with talons as they grasped his prey. Wings protruded from his back as his legs retracted into his body. With a beat of his wings, he pulled the dwarves out of the large window and up in the air, screaming.

They flew hard and fast towards a small island far from the shore of Midgard. The brothers were released from the eagle's talons near a rocky land that was only visible when the seas were low. They plunged beneath the surface but scrambled to land. Their splashing gained the attention of the Jotun king from the deep. Neither brother could escape, so their panic rose as fast as the tides as the giant eagle circled above.

The night was at its darkest and the dawn was quickly approaching. They not only had the fear of drowning but also the sunrise meant danger to the vampires. They pleaded to the night sky, begging the eagle to spare them. They even called to me, but I did what I could by sending Sigurd their way.

"We'll give you riches! We'll give you anything you want!" The brothers yelled at the eagle.

The giant eagle swooped down and perched next to the brothers. "Riches? I do not need riches," said the Jotun. "I want revenge!"

Fjalar and Galar shuffled their feet as far from the water's edge as they could, looking at each other afraid. "We can give you the mead of poetry. It replenishes your body and prolongs life. It gives you a great talent of wordsmithing and great wisdom in the art of word arrangement to control others' actions without realising they are being controlled," the brothers pleaded with the eagle, hoping the Jotun would show mercy.

"Wisdom, you say. I need wisdom," the eagle pondered and plotted a much larger plan of revenge, not toward the brothers but towards myself.

The brothers desperately gave the location of the three vats without Thyazi asking in an attempt to further sway him into showing mercy. It was to no avail. When the eagle left, he planned never to return to save them. The night waned on and the sunrise cause the horizon to appear on fire. The sea was steadily rising, and the island was shrinking little by little.

If the sun rose and touched their skin, they would be turned stone and sink to the bottom of the water, never to be seen again. The brothers scrambled frantically, shouting and screaming for help. Luckily for them, my son needed to find the way back to Asgard, or I would have left them also and neglected their cries that floated on the air.

Aegir decided to show them mercy but had to wait until the sea claimed them before he could take them down to serve in his hall. They were too consumed by the fear of death to even dare to challenge him as he was the powerful Jotun king of the oceans.

In the dark of the night, the spray of the sea was hitting their face and survival seemed bleak as the water's edge touched their toes. The brothers heard a raven's call. Wiping their eyes, they spotted a ship heading in their direction. The captain manoeuvred his boat near the island's edge and raised his sword against Aegir, who was thigh deep in the bitter sea. "Jotun! The brothers are coming with me!" the captain declared. "I have slain the mighty dragon called Fafnir, and my blade does not fear you."

Aegir looked curiously at the captain. "Who are you?" he asked while staring closely at the markings on his helmet.

"I am Sigurd, King of the Volsungs. And I need to find my way home!" Upon Sigurd's declaration, Aegir recognised the markings and left willingly. Aegir could not harm Sigurd due to an oath he took to enchant the helmet.

Luckily for the brothers, I provided the support needed. The longer time they spent on troubled waters, the more likely it would have led to their loss forever. Winds can change instantly, taking you to and from safe shores.

Sigurd allowed the brothers to board his ship, thus also providing shelter from the sun, and granted them safe passage to the mainland. He provided shelter from the sun's rays. In return, they shared the details only gained by drinking Kvasir's to reveal the way to Asgard. Their eyes had haunted his sleep from the time he spotted them creeping on his castle's walls, but due to his rescue, they swore off blood for sustenance. Once the brothers realised their blood thirst would attract unwanted attention, they decided to open a tavern and continue with creating great magical items. They returned to the forge and bellows, and their work would become legend. They became Brokkr and Eitri, and they also became more cautious of those that came to their door.

The giant eagle returned home. It wasn't Thyazi but Suttung in disguise. His plans were to steal wisdom and keep it out of my hands. His love was high up among the stars pulling the sun across the skies, ever faithful to the noble duty she chose that provides life to everyone. Perhaps I'll reunite them when the day was right, but first, I required that mead and I would get it back by any means necessary.

# Heavy is the Head

Suttung could have his victory for a time as we had Idunn and her golden apples to prolong our youth and fight the effects of the aging process. Honir remained in the cells of Vanaheim, but I needed him to return to Asgard. The great and noble Honir was imprisoned due to the discovery of him pretending to be worthy of leadership. I took up the task with Geri and Freki and we travelled to a ship enclosure that was very unique. Loki and I were driven to purpose. We were driven to purpose with our loyalty to Heimdall. His son needed to come home and no god should remain in chains, especially one so influential in times to come.

We approached a unique set of docks in Midgard called Nóatún. There was a weary old fisherman stood at the edge of the pier with a fishing pole in hand. I approached with my wolves by my side. The breeze was cool, and the spray of the crashing waves cooled me on the warm summer's day. "Nice day for the fish," I said to the old fisherman.

"Not today. They must sense the presence of your wolves. They don't like them, and neither do I," he replied.

"Thankfully for you and them, they aren't much for swimming." I paused. "It was wise to give them an early meal before visiting you since I usually require a feast for the price of my presence," I suggested to the fisherman.

"Perhaps I'll use them as bait?" He replied unflinchingly at the wolves growling and snarling at his back. I raised my hand to bring Geri and Freki to a halt.

"Let's drop the charade, Njord. It is quick to make an enemy on a short twisted, crooked path. I want you as a true friend, so the path is long, but I wish it to be straightforward," I said, tired of the pretence.

"Honir, *he* is why you bother to grace me with your presence. His freedom will come at a great price. Let me think," Njord paused, pretending to think of a fair value. "Sumarbrandr. Yes, that will be the fee of Honir's release."

I sent Geri and Freki to retrieve an ox, watching them snap at each other in their hunt for a feast, while I continued to barter with the king of Vanaheim. I turned back to Njord. "As if not proclaiming your only son king of the elves wasn't enough?" I reached into my grey cloak, slowly drawing out Vili's old sword. The metal gleamed as the sun hit the blade. It symbolised confidence, slaying many of the undead during the Great War. Njord's eyes lit up when he saw the sword.

"Give it here and I'll send for Honir's release at once." I reluctantly handed it over, knowing I'd reclaim it back one day.

An hour of uncomfortable silence had passed until Honir appeared gasping from beneath the waves. He scrambled to climb the pier and feverishly crawled onto the boardwalk. "Take Heimdall's boy and go Odin. Vanaheim will be with you if you should need it. You have my word," Njord said while admiring his new weapon.

"I will not outstay my welcome, friend. Respect will turn to duty, and both will be lost forever as time continues," I said as I helped Honir to his feet. We left Nóatún to find Loki and I knew just where to go.

Arriving at a campfire, Loki was preparing a fresh kill of oxen, the meat already on the embers of a fire. "I've been cooking the meat for a while now, Odin. A feasssst worthy of the mighty Honir to celebrate hissss freedom," Loki informed us. I grabbed a piece of the meat but could feel that it was still raw. I looked at Loki, disappointed. He seemed genuine, but through some form of trickery, the beef wasn't cooking. This caused me to lose my appetite and to decide to scout ahead, leaving Honir and Loki to prepare the food.

High above, there was an eagle circling Loki's fresh kill. It waited until I left the camp before descending on the two.

"I can help you cook it if you'd like? But you'll have to share," The eagle offered. Loki was a friend trying to impress me but sharing the great feast with a Jotun eagle caused him concern. He looked suspiciously at the bird but recalled my look of disappointment at the lack of cooked ox. He agreed, still cautious of the bird's intent.

With a beat of the eagle's wings, the winds picked up. What was once tiny embers on the coals was now blazing fire. Loki gained a quick friend as the fire burned hot. It wouldn't be long before time waned on, and the friendship was proven untrue.

Before long, the meat was cooked, and the three began feasting, tearing the meat from the bone. Loki's greedy nature ended up getting the better of him as he began to swat the eagle away, aggravating it. When I returned, I spotted the two of them squabbling.

The fastest of friends may fall out when a meal is shared. It was and always will be a shame for a guest to dispute with a guest. I immediately realised not all was as it appeared. I threw my spear, hitting the bird on his side. He screeched out in pain and began to grow in size. The eagle increased and expanded, tripling the size of Loki and the rest of us. With my spear still in his side, he clutched Loki in his talons. Beating its wings, it rose in the air causing great gusts knocking Honir and me off our feet.

The eagle soared high above the clouds, causing Loki to become terrified. "What do you want!" Loki screamed over the turbulent air rushing past.

"I can't have the one I love, so Odin's demise will suffice. I will watch him suffer the slow death, and I will drink to his wretched bones," the eagle vowed.

"PUT ME DOWN!!!! SAFELY!!!" Loki screamed at the eagle and was tortured most cruelly. He was dropped and allowed to freefall to his death, only to be collected before he impacted the ground.

"If you aid me in my revenge, I will allow you to go free," the eagle finally offered. Loki was out of options. The chance of escape was low, and survival seemed impossible. He agreed, unaware that I would be able to use this opportunity to gain the mead of poetry. That would mean the plan had to be executed perfectly, given this was my only chance, and Loki's participation was required.

"I'm Thyazi and I want the apples of Idunn, little Loki," Suttung said, hiding his true identity.

"How? I mean, it's not as if the gods won't realise their source of long life is gone," Loki pondered.

"You seem smart enough to figure it out. You have three days. Bring her to me. I will wait for you on the ash tree in Jotunheim," Suttung flapped his great wings again, carrying him off into the sky. Loki began his long journey back to Asgard with thoughts of stealing Idunn.

When Loki returned, his face was filled with dread, fear and shame. I knew what Suttung desired without him revealing anything. I simply put my hand on his shoulder and eased his thoughts. "Do what you have to do, Loki," I said. He never said a word and just set his mind on his purpose.

# Best Laid Plans

Later that evening, Loki approached Idunn. "Oh Idunn, I feel awful. My backaches and my knees are sore. May I please have one of your delicious golden apples?" Idunn looked at Loki, scanning his outward appearance for signs of aging.

"You don't look old, Loki. Is this a game or a trick?" Idunn inquired curiously about the nature of Loki's visit.

"I hide my ageing well, but I too bring concerning news. There is word from Jotunheim that your applesss have begun to grow there," Loki slyly informed her.

"This cannot be, unless a chance of fate or a Jotun has salvaged seeds from our scraps. Either way, we must destroy the tree. Come with me, Loki, and we shall tear the tree down together," Idunn said, determined to restore order in the realms.

They gathered up a few supplies and left for Jotunheim in a hurry. In the cover of darkness, they travelled far. Along the way, Idunn revealed to Loki about the time we shared. She spoke about my looks in my younger years and described me as handsome as Baldur.

The sun rose on the third day as they reached the ash tree in Jotunheim. "This is no apple tree, Loki. You deceived me, but why?" Idunn asked as the winds began to pick up. Loki remained quiet while something circled them in the sky. The shadow from something above became larger until Loki and Idunn were consumed by darkness. With a mighty thud, Suttung landed, and grasping Idunn, he turned and looked at Loki.

"Your oath is fulfilled, Loki," he said before he expanded his wings and took off with Idunn terrified n his talons. She struggled and vowed to one day cause him great pain for his treachery.

Loki returned to Asgard, and for a time, everything went unnoticed. The years went on before the gods called a meeting concerned about the effects of ageing and the absence of Idunn. The council of gods had become a group of old men and women by then. Grey hairs were sprinkled throughout everyone's appearance, and the struggle of wrestling old age was on our faces.

"Allfather, who is behind this? Where is Idunn?" They all asked.

"Loki did it," I replied.

"I should break him until he tells me where she is. And if she's harmed…" Thor threatened as he trailed off his anger.

"She is unharmed, boy," I declared. Just then, Loki walked in late to the meeting with a nervous look on his face. The gods turned their attention to Loki's entrance.

"We know what you've done, Loki," Njord said.

"You had better return her, Loki. Make up for what you have done," Heimdall said with a booming voice. Loki's face looked around desperately for a solution.

After watching him squirm, I decided to provide Loki with a solution. "I will gift you with two spells and a distraction, oath brother." The spells I gave were the ability for him to take the shape of a squirrel and to transform things into acorns to avoid suspicion.

It was my plan all along as soon as Loki was taken. I knew Suttung and what he wanted, and I knew he'd use Loki to get it. The blood of Kvasir would be returned to his empty carcass. My body was old and weak, and my warrior's ability was drastically reduced with my missing eye. This mead would make me cunning and powerful without my physical prowess.

"Leave in three days, Loki. That'll allow me to create a distraction for you to return Idunn. Freya, I will need a wet stone like no other and a drill to bore into the deepest and hardest of rock and stone," I requested.

"Here, take Rati. No rock is too hard or stone too thick. Take this whetstone. One slide across any metal, and it will make the blade as sharp as Excalibur," my love replied, handing me the tools I needed.

"Thank you, my lady," I said to her, forcing a smile on her face.

"Do what you need to, my love," she replied, giving me a cold shiver down my old back. It was as if she knew something I didn't, which gave me a terrible feeling in my stomach.

I took the supplies I needed and left for Suttung's kingdom. To attack it directly would have been foolish instead of using his weakness: his desires of vengeance.

I approached a Jotun's farm with caution, as there were many giant slaves in the fields. I put their number around nine. These giant, clumsy Jotuns were working away with scythes slashing at the year's crops. It was midday, and the sun was at its hottest. The nine massive farm workers stopped for a break. That's when I made my move.

I stopped on a hill just in range for the Jotun workers to see. I stripped myself of all my clothes and lightly dressed two posts as heroes but naked; they were not. The art of deception is to manipulate thoughts through visual input enhanced with verbal description. I proceeded down the hill with my plan in my head and the whetstone in my sack. This part of the story was proof it is better to have a sharp wit than being simply confident in your blades ability to cut.

"How can you work away all day with blunt blades? Farm work is hard enough without making it harder with poor tools," I said to the group of giants resting in the sun.

"Who are you, naked old man? Who are your friends on top of the hill? And what do you know of our blades?" One of the workers had risen with his scythe threateningly moving towards me as I spoke.

"I am Bölverk, a fitting name, for if anyone was brave enough to challenge me my friends on the hill would be swift to avenge me. Sigurd, the dragon slayer and Thor are slayers of trolls, ogres and giants. Bad things are fated for those that wish me harm. However, if you'll let me, I can help," I said, pulling the whetstone from my bag. I ran it across the blade three times and handed the scythe back to the giant. The edge was sharp, and the giant slashed the crops with much more ease.

Upon seeing this, the rest of the giant workers rose from their break and desired the whetstone for themselves.

I sharpened every blade and offered a challenge while feeding each servant's ego. "You are the biggest. You must be the leader. You can slice quicker, but *you* can carry more," I said to the suspicious giants. I shared a laugh but not my thoughts. The giants' attempt to kill me before would be equally returned. "Gather round and get close. I'll throw the stone in the air, and whoever catches it will keep it for the rest of their life." Huddled so close together, I threw the stone in the air. They never realised that it would be with their own sharpened scythes that cut each of them down. One ogre gained his victory as his brothers lay dead around him. He celebrated, not realising that those he worked with so closely were no more. I magically turned my staff back into a spear and plunged it through his chest, ending his life instantly. I kept true to my word. He did possess the stone for the rest of his life.

I picked up the stone and retrieved my clothes from the posts. Once I had them back on, I headed towards Baugi's place. Baugi was Suttung's little brother charged with the harvesting of crops to supply the king's hall. Word travelled fast that his servants had died before they could harvest them. It was lucky it was only it was only the news of their deaths and not the means behind the tragedy. "What to do? what to do?" Baugi asked himself, pacing the floor. I knocked on his door and provided a solution to his woes.

"Greetings, Baugi, I have heard of your woes, and I will provide some wisdom first before providing a solution. The wise should know how to save for harsher times. No one truly knows when it will be upon them. No need to lie awake at night with worry, Baugi. It should bring you joy to know I will complete the harvest in a day. I will do the work of nine giants providing solution to your problems in exchange for a sip of the mead of poetry," I said, setting the terms. Baugi paced, trying to find a way out of his current predicament.

"Haha! Your clothes are torn, and your shoes are worn. How can I believe you can complete such great feats?" Baugi mocked.

"As long as someone is washed and fed, their clothes do not determine their worth. I have done much work and travelled far. I am not ashamed of the clothes I wear," I replied.

"The mead is not mine to give, strange wanderer, but I'm sure if you provide aid, my brother might accommodate you with what you need. What is your name?" Baugi asked.

"I am Bölverk, Gilling's son, and if you get me an audience with your brother, I can earn the drink," I said confidently. Often, I come to many either too early or too late. After all is discovered, or too early to realise. Knowledge is unpopular and cannot please."

"Grab rest, old man. Your work begins at daybreak," Baugi said, guiding me to my resting quarters.

# Deceiving Gunlodd

The next day I woke early before Sol had dragged the sun to rise. I had my desires on another's property, and there is no victory for a lazy wolf. The sleeper is seldom victorious. With few servants and much work, I would have failed if I had slept late. Success is won by those that work swiftly.

With the dead giants' sharpened scythes, I created a machine of sticks and pulley systems to make the work easier for my old bones to manage. I had the job completed before the evening, much to Baugi's surprise, who was in awe of my efforts. I told him of the machine created and offered it as a gift if he swore an oath to help me gain access to the mead. He agreed, now that Baugi didn't require servants anymore, he could manage the work on the farm without relying on the aid of many.

I'd been staying with Baugi and on the third day, he and I left for his brother's castle as Loki left Asgard for Idunn's rescue. We reached Suttung's throne room, and Baugi began to plead my case to acquire a sip of the magical mead.

Suttung appeared different than before, much more powerful than the mighty eagle he once was. Baugi stuttered and fumbled with his words, intimidated by his brother.

"Let the hosts with guests be glad and merry. Modest they should be but talk well if they want to be seen as wise. Stuttering and mumbling around your equal, great Baugi, will allow them to think you a fool," I said to my companion being sure that Suttung was in earshot. After that, I remained quiet in his court. Allowing others to discuss my case earned me nothing. But it would be my sweet word to Gunlodd that would win me my prize.

Suttung looked upon my aged form with familiarity. "Bölverk, you look like someone I used to know. You will have no drink of mead and you will grow old and die with the rest of your gods, Odin!" He snapped at me while the room remained shocked at the revelation. I remained reserved, not wasting speech or breath on meaningless words. If I had talked too much at the table, I might have revealed my real plan. It was then that Baugi and I left the throne room. I knew where I was unwelcome.

"Remember your oath," I said quietly to the king's brother as we went.

As soon as we left the castle, we made our descent down the mountain. "That'll do," Baugi said, stopping our decline. Beneath our feet was a strange and beautiful song. "My niece, Gunlodd, is trapped beneath us. It was such a shame she was tasked to protect the mead alone. She has been there since she came of age," he began sharing the details of the poor girl's duties and her origin. She was the child of Suttung and Idunn and was the greatest of warriors with strength and skill to surpass Thor. She was the perfect choice as the protector of the mead, but her weakness was her isolation.

I handed the drill called Rati to Baugi to begin his aid to the access to the mead. He expressed his hatred of my deception and began to plot to kill me once I had access through the mountain's surface. My all-seeing eye and foresight could envision his actions before they could come to pass. "I'm done," Baugi huffed and puffed, exhausted from boring. I leant over and blew into the hole. The breath returned with a face full of dust and I looked to Baugi disappointed with his lies.

"Not yet, Baugi. There is still more to be done." He mumbled under his breath at me before he began boring with the drill again. The mumbling told me he had ill intent for me, and it continued until he broke through.

"I'm done now!" He said, raising his voice in frustration. I leant over to blow in the hole again. No dust blew back on me, and I heard Baugi move toward me with the drill pointing at my back. I avoided the stabbing before returning my spear through his heart. I then quickly transformed into a snake and made my way into the narrow passage through the mountain. If I had taken the long road to the entry, I would have likely lost my head. Suttung would have increased his guards and even the attempt to access conventionally would have been foolish.

I slithered towards the beautiful song into the depths of the mountain. My mind raced of thoughts on how to manoeuvre Gunlodd. Then it suddenly came to me, a plan I knew I would regret. Thankfully, the words of my Freya reassured my concerns with it.

Upon breaching the hole, I took the shape of my son, Sigurd. He was handsome, and all races admired him. It was the perfect disguise. Knowing it might come back to bite me one day, I made one alteration to my look. My feet bore the resemblance of another king. I knew that the beauty of my appearance would drop the guard of the feisty maiden. As she looked upon my form, I noticed her spear lowering slightly. Gunlodd became enchanted as her spear fell further.

"Speak, beautiful stranger. Why are you here, and what is your name?" She asked with a beautiful sparkle in her eyes whose shine would rival that of the stars. They resembled her father's.

"I...I, Forget," I said like herons were hovering above a feast, unable to use words while gazing at Gunlodd's beauty. "My name is Baldur, and word has spread around the nine realms of your beauty. I had to see if the rumours held. Sadly, they do not compare close to what I see now. Such beauty can't be described by anyone that hasn't gained the magical insight from Óðrœrir. If I was allowed a sip, I could speak of your loveliness to everyone else," I said as her smile widened, and her cheeks lifted. It wasn't long before we made it to her bed chambers. I'll spare the details but let's say after three times she was spent. I would not have survived without Gunlodd's help. I was almost too comfortable with her warm embrace. I regretted using her in that way, but my true love was waiting for me at home. As the sunlight hit her pillow, she woke to an empty bed as I made my escape to provide Loki with his chance to rescue the mead of poetry and Idunn.

A drink of the marvellous mead I was gifted, and in return, I gave heartbreak. That night I lost respect and trust from the Jotun race through my actions with Gunlodd. She would become the sole heir of Jotunheim, though she preferred the solitude of the mountains. She told everyone of my deeds and transgressions before exiling herself from her own kingdom. What I gained, though, I have used to hone my wisdom. I would use the remainder to revive Kvasir with Óðrœrir the sacred draught.

Gunlodd left her station, no longer a prisoner of her duties, to report to Suttung of her failure. He was enraged and cast her from the kingdom before he took to his mutated eagle form, the body of a mighty lion, but his head still that of an eagle, and began his hunt.

Upon returning to her chambers, she watched as the small mammal scampered away carrying several acorns, an act Gunlodd easily dismissed. That was until she realised the three vats were gone. "Ratatoskr!!!!" She exclaimed as Loki made his escape in his squirrel form.

Furious with a second failure, she left her post intending to sit upon her father's throne and await his return. She needed to let him know what had happened so that proper measures could be put in place to reobtain what was taken.

She wandered the harsh lands of Jotunheim in the cold and though her heart may have been frozen like her surroundings, she seethed and burned with hatred.

Along the way, she spotted a cave and decided to take shelter. Upon settling in and being alone with her thoughts, she had inadvertently pushed herself to a point of never coming back. Gunlodd died that day in the cave, and as a result, something terrifying was created. She became determined to gain the prize of a godly husband and would relentlessly pursue her goals. In the end, the final result was a self-sufficient hunter that none in all the nine realms could escape once she homed in on them. She became Skadi, the winter Jotun of hunting and skiing, and would one day make Asgard pay for my betrayal. There is no wrath that can compare with a woman scorned.

# The Star on the Tree

It wasn't long before the great eagle king spotted his prey. I was in falcon form, flying as swiftly as possible, but unfortunately, the Griffin could fly faster. I zoomed low, weaving through forests and mountains, attempting to evade him before making it to the sea. "You took my wife, Odin! You took my love!" He screamed over the rush of air. Hurricanes began to appear from the skies as we flew. His rage was causing great destruction on the lands below while forcing me to adapt to the situation. I had to think quickly. I flew further towards the centre of the ocean, keeping low.

The winds were in pursuit, close behind Suttung's furious flapping. Cyclones and typhoons filled the air with moisture. I weaved swiftly between them, trying to keep their effects from as many sailors as I could.

The ocean's spray dampened our feathers, and I knew immediately I needed to change forms if I intended on escaping with my prize. I transformed swiftly into a penguin and dove into the waters below, narrowly escaping Suttung's great talons. I breached the surface every few moments to get him closer to the water.

His wings became heavy due to the water slowing him down a little. I decided to next transform back into a falcon, intending to lose the moisture in my feathers and gain distance between us. "It was Sol's choice to leave you!" I yelled back at him. He shook his feathers and began to gain speed once more. There was no reasoning with him. Suttung was out for blood. "You want her so bad! I'll take you to her!"

I flew up, straight up. Winds rushed, and gravity pulled, but I flapped my wings harder than ever through the mist of the clouds where visibility was low. I turned to look to see if Suttung was following when I heard his eagle call as his silhouette appeared behind me. I continued my rushed pace until I breached the clouds. Once I had, it was so peaceful, the thin air made it euphoric. The light blue atmosphere provided me with calm. Suttung couldn't use his magic manipulation of the winds this high up.

Suttung was just out of reach from clutching me in his talons. I remained focused on flying as high as I could in order to breach the atmosphere. I needed to get him to his wife as soon as I could despite his rampant pursuit.

Just then, I could hear the trampling of a horse's footsteps. I smiled as I saw the chariot headed towards us just before I dropped momentarily out of consciousness due to low air supply. This caused me to return to my human form, effectively falling straight down. As the griffin's claws enlarged preparing to catch his prey, something beautiful distracted him for a moment which allowed me to slip between his fingers. He paused, surprised to see such a sight, and in the process, caught a glimpse of his wife.

Sol was galloping toward him with the sun close behind, a warm smile gracing her beautiful face. She did not slow as she knew the wolf was in pursuit. She waved at him to get out of the way, but his joy made him blind to the danger being towed behind her.

He swooped to dodge the eight horse's hooves and chariot from crushing him. As they continued to gallop, he looked at his wife from behind, making him lost in the moment. Soon after, he felt the sun beginning to scorch his feathers to nothingness. As he began to fall to his death, he tried in vain to flap his featherless wings, never taking his eyes from his fleeting lover.

I had returned to Asgard to find Loki with the three vats and Idunn safely home. She restored the gods to their glorious youth, and all was momentarily good, until a comet-like object plunged into Asgard, just metres away, leaving a massive crater in its wake. That crater would later become a great lake to which my steed would usually exist, but that story is for another time. Upon closer observation, we realized it was Suttung, alive but barely.

I took all I had to approach him and plunge my spear through his slowing heart. I regretted having to expedite his death in this manner. Given what a noble enemy he was, he deserved to go as swiftly as possible. I then reached down to his charred remains and plucked his eye out to replace the one I lost. In doing so, I regained greater vision once more.

I then chose to ceremonially burn his body. It was the right thing to do. He was a king of nobility, and his death was my fault. I began to speak the enchanted words that echoed in Asgard. The winds would rise again. From beneath the flames of the griffin's corpse, he rose from the ashes. Suttung's spirit spread its wings. Dripping with fire and burning as bright as the sun, I asked for his forgiveness. He looked at his new glorious form and smiled. "Odin, why did you grant me this power?"

"I did this to honour you. I have done you a disservice, and this has the only way I knew to right it," I replied, feeling the heat from his Phoenix form.

"How?" he asked, puzzled.

"Fly, my friend. High up beyond the blue skies into the vastness of Ginnungagap. There, one day, Sol will return to you with your Daughter," I said with a joyful tear, for my foe turned to a friend.

"Gunlodd?" he asked.

"Go fly now—due North. Become the north star, a guiding light in the darkest nights. Goodbye, my friend. Be with the one you love," I said, mustering a smile. With a flash of burning bright light, he was gone, and I retired to the feasting hall, where the gods gathered in celebration of my victory.

"That wasss impressive, Odin," hissed Loki.

"Do not use that spell, Loki. I sent Suttung far from the mortals, boy. He cannot harm them where he is. The dead must remain dead unless used to guide the living—a beacon of hope from afar or a navigation tool to keep them on track. They should never directly interfere with the living," I said to him sternly. Unfortunately, it was in Loki's greedy nature to test limits or even ignore them completely.

I returned to the festivities and took a few more mouthfuls of the mead of Kvasir's blood as I joined in celebration. Suddenly, with a rush of power, I became intoxicated with wisdom. Wisdom wasn't the only change I felt upon consuming this concoction, though. There were several other side effects including a loss of appetite for food that was replaced by bloodlust and having my senses heightened far beyond that of Heimdall's. I now could smell the scent of hate on my enemy's breath and my words became a weapon to soothe any of them. I could hear the mockery in their tone. I could sense the flutter of a maiden's heart beneath her breast at the words I spoke.

As a side effect due to Loki's blood oath, my form transformed also. My heightened senses came with a beastly state. The head of a wolf, with claws to match. The body of a man but with the strength that'll rival most gods. However, each time I took this form, my bones broke, causing bloodcurdling pain and anguish. It was as if I was made stronger through the pain.

I took this power back to Valhöll to share with my Einherjar. Each day they will fight to keep their position in my ranks, and if they fell, Hel would collect them. If they proved themselves loyal and worthy, I gave them a sip of the mead that changed me. After their drink, they would receive the bite transforming them into Ulfhednar. My wolves also benefited when they proved themselves worthy of a drink: when they were injured, they would heal from their wounds and rise again to prove their might and readiness for Ragnarök.

In the days that followed, the Yeti clan of Jotuns came to what was once Suttung's hall to ask Gunlodd of Bölverk. They wondered if I had made it back to Asgard or if Suttung had his kill. I knew I would one day face the consequences of my actions. I would have to make amends for the ones I have hurt and those who have died. Losing all Jotun trust by lying at the feast and breaking Gunlodd's heart was unwise but necessary. Rarely was a king without conscience when dealing with matters out of his control.

Loki kept the spell of the squirrel and made alterations to it himself. He could transform into any animal he wished using his garments. This magic would be a helpful trick in times to come, but that is a story for another time.

Under the cover of darkness, I collected the body of Kvasir. Far from prying eyes, I returned the remainder of the blood from the three vats to Kvasir's empty corpse. Once it had been absorbed and he awoke, he was different. He was more predatorial and less of the wandering, peaceful human he used to be. Like the Strigoi, he developed a thirst for blood, and it sustained his immortality. His wisdom far surpassed my own as he returned from the dead.

No longer the man he was, he desired isolation and decided to live as a hermit from then on in the castle near Transylvania. He now only wanted to sleep for centuries at a time and would end up going by many names. He would only wake to feed when he needed it.

One such name was Bragi, the master of poetry. He charmed many a fair maiden, but his immortality won the heart of Idunn. He would not need her apples to remain young. She, therefore, knew their love was true.

# The Riddle Weaver

After much conflict over the years, I decided to visit my wise uncle once more. Much time had passed since the resurrection of his head. His wit was sharp with the constant updates from the fluid he drank from his well. With the ear of Heimdall and an all-seeing eye, he knew everything in all the realms. However, when you remain confined to a space for a long time, you become twisted in nature.

The flames on the torches within the cave seemed duller than before. I stepped into the grim area of the well cautiously. "I knew you would come, Odin," Mimir boasted. "I grow tired of our usual exchanges. How about a wager this time? My head or yours? If I win, your head will join mine, removed by Vidar. And if you win, my head will go with you. What do you say, Odin?" I paused for a moment, but there was much I had to learn.

"Such serious stakes, uncle, but I will play your game."

An eery silence filled the cave as Mimir smile widened. "I'll start, young wolf. Let's see, ah yes. Loki's child, the one that roams free. What is his name in Australia?" Mimir asked.

"Ah...starting with a trick question, clever Mimir. Borlung, Dhakkan, Kajura, Goorialla, Kunmanggur, Ngalyod, Numereji, Taipan, Tulloun, Wagyl, Wanamangura, Witij. He is more commonly known as the rainbow serpent, the bringer of rain, because Thor seeks him out, but he always evades him, that slippery snake. My question is, is there a way to change Thor's fate?" I replied. Mimir's eyes blazed like bright red embers.

"Fate cannot be changed. What has been written can only be delayed, not stopped? Since you answered well, I will give you a heads up. When Thor goes fishing, make sure his line is frayed." Though he could see my pause to think on his words, he pressed on with another question.

"What is the serpent called when spotted in other waters around Midgard?" he asked, enjoying his little game.

"It goes by many names and confused by many survivors trying to explain it. It has been described as a dragon, a monster and once was mistaken as a white whale." his grin turned to a frown.

"Answer the question!" Mimir's voice boomed deep in the bellows of the cave.

"Loch Ness monster, Shenlong, Ryujin, Bakunawa, Kukulkan, Apophis and Ketos to say a few wise Mimir. But time goes on, and it is too precious to waste talking about names." Mimir agreed to allow me to return a question.

"What happens when I die at Ragnarök?" I asked.

"You know your end lies in the jaws of a wolf. Beyond that, my aid will avenge you. He will tear your killer into pieces. He will require a boot to protect him. The shoes should be made from recycled leather so he can step on Fenrir's bottom jaw," he explained. I was taken back by his words, but he had come back from the dead. He had nothing to gain from lying because of my new abilities. I'd be able to detect deception, after all, why would he have ulterior motives?

"Ok, dear nephew, where, in Midgard, will Jormungandr's headrest when it finally meets its tail?" He tested.

"That is challenging, uncle. Jormungandr's head will be located in the...Bermuda triangle," I said confidently. "What of Loki and his involvement in Ragnarök?" I asked, probing for possible events I could influence.

"Your oath to your brothers will keep him safe and your reliance on him will be your downfall, boy," Mimir said. "He will accomplish much for the gods, but his duality will lead to his undoing," Mimir answered.

"Ok, let's move on to your nemesis. Fenrir is now the ninth realm, a gateway to the home of the dead. His body is a mountainous landscape. What will the name of the highest peak be?" Mimir quizzed.

"People who go to Helheim are provided rest and warmth from the coldness of Niflheim. A gateway between life and death provides a veil between both. Only those near death or on the brink can come back and speak of those already passed, but the highest peak of wolf mountain is called Everest," I replied. "Now my question, uncle, what are the fates of my sons?" Mimir's eyes flashed again for longer this time.

"Tyr will share your fate. Thor's greatest victory will be his doom. Hödr's son will kill him. Baldur will die by an oath brother and blood brother. The fates have decreed, Allfather," Mimir proclaimed. His words haunted my soul.

"Final question Allfather, and that'll be a riddle. What has a cap but no head? A foot but no leg?" Mimir riddled.

"Ah, cunning riddle weaver," I said, stalling for a minute while pacing around the dreary cave. I repeated the puzzle over and over to myself. I thought a human with no legs, but that's not cryptic enough. I thought of Mimir if I gave him a hat, but he was not fond of humour in his current position. Then it came to me, "a mountain!!!!" I exclaimed, happy to have found the answer.

"Ah yes, Allfather, well done. Now you better make this a hard one, or there will be a stalemate." I thought long and hard about it. The silence in the well was deafening. What can he not know? He could hear what happened, but the future could be uncertain.

"When Baldur dies and is placed on the funeral pyre, what will I whisper in his ear?" the look of panic ran across his face. He started bumbling and stuttering as he postponed his delivery of an answer. moments turned to minutes, and still, Mimir couldn't procure a response.

"You win, but in a way, we both do," he said, happy to have lost the competition.

"How so wise, Mimir?" I asked.

"Vidar and I can come to Asgard and leave this wretched cave behind," Mimir answered back. It was as if he wished to lose the game all along.

I grabbed his head and called Vidar, who was tending the gardens. We all headed home as Huginn and Muninn flew overhead. Mimir's old dwelling was now vacant. Well, at least for the moment.

When the door of the ash tree in the garden opened, Verdandi's fingers crawled from beyond the doorway. Niflheim was open, and she still knew how to hold a grudge. She'd had time to plot and knew where to hit me to make it hurt. She would aim at my children.

"I will get you where you caused me so much suffering, Odin. An eye for an eye," she vowed as she plucked my eye from Mimir's well.

It was a long journey back in the dead of winter's night. The howling of wolves echoed throughout the distant forests. All kinds of creatures stirred from Jotunheim to Midgard.

Something or someone was moving in the darkness, and I could smell a familiar scent in the air. Footsteps crunching the snow caused wildlife to succumb to silence. It was Skadi, and she hadn't gained help from Verdandi yet.

As she approached, I changed our appearance to three wise, old men seeking rest from the perilous Jotunheim. She walked on, deeming us not worthy of her time or anger. She travelled in the darkness toward Mimir's well, towards Verdandi's plots and magics. That would be the regretful inspiration for Verdandi's attempt to destroy Asgard. She would empower already powerful Jotuns to destroy us; a great threat in the coming times and Asgard would be made stronger through Verdandi's challenges.

On our way through Midgard, we left word for the mortals to make shoes. The offerings to Vidar would consist of leftover scraps from each one. The offerings would be helpful for the most significant war yet to come—the Ragnarök.

Now comes the end to this part of my tale. These are the runes that wrote my story that I share with you, good host. Times of failure and triumph, each moment a gift of wisdom; times that could have killed me and brought Ragnarök closer and times that I rose and delayed it that little bit longer.

Life itself is an interesting ride on the branches of Yggdrasil but best keep your runes to yourself to not be exploited. A secret to one person is wise. A secret to two comes with risk. To three is foolish as all will know, and none can be trusted.

Thank you for sacrificing your time and attention to this weary, old man. Your hospitality has been generous, but I must be going. Unfortunately, time stands still for no man or god for that matter.

Perhaps our path might cross again, and I can tell you tales of the heroes of Asgard, tales of trolls and ogres, giants and golems. Many stories of monsters from myths and the gods that defeated them all.

# ABOUT THE AUTHOR

My journey as a writer is probably not remarkable or noteworthy to most. I am a simple man that discovered paganism and thought why. After learning and deciphering a lot, I discovered a healthy religion for understanding life balance. I wrote my book sentence by sentence any chance I got. Possible kennings, metaphors and links inspire each character's evolution with veneration and worship, according to archaeological finds. My life has its difficulties, just like yours. Trying to maintain a work-life balance isn't without its own challenges. Life happens, and it was up to me to adapt to it the best way I could. I worked 10–11-hour shifts, studying and trying to be a present father and husband. Life isn't easy, but nothing worth having ever is.

Printed in Great Britain
by Amazon